THE WHITE FOX CHRONICLES

THE WHITE FOX CHRONICLES

ESCAPE
★
RETURN
★
BREAKOUT

GARY PAULSEN

DELACORTE PRESS

Published by
Delacorte Press
an imprint of
Random House Children's Books
a division of
Random House, Inc.
1540 Broadway
New York, New York 10036

Visit us on the Web! www.randomhouse.com/kids
Educators and librarians, for a variety of teaching tools, visit us at
www.randomhouse.com/teachers

Library of Congress Cataloging-in-Publication Data
Cataloging-in-Publication Data is available from the Library of Congress.
ISBN 0-385-32254-2

The text of this book is set in 12-point Goudy.

Manufactured in the United States of America

June 2000

10 9 8 7 6 5 4 3 2

QPB

CONTENTS

Book One: ESCAPE   1

Book Two: RETURN   99

Book Three: BREAKOUT   193

ESCAPE

CHAPTER 1

Fourteen-year-old Cody Pierce stopped hoeing the rectangular patch of dirt the camp guards called a vegetable garden. Nothing really edible grew in it anyway and the weeds could wait.

Something was up. He could feel it. The tower guards were standing at full attention and those on the ground were edging toward the main buildings.

The camp commander, Colonel Sidoron, burst through the door of his office, buttoning the shirt of his green army fatigues. An aide ran along beside him holding up a mirror. Sidoron looked in it quickly, ran his hand through his short black beard and then brushed the aide aside.

The lanky white-blond boy in the vegetable garden leaned on his hoe, watching the bustle through gray eyes.

A U.S. Army utility vehicle with a CCR flag painted over the white star on the door boiled down the dirt road toward the prison camp. It was followed by a transport truck and another utility vehicle.

Two guards ran to open the wooden gates. The three vehicles sped into the compound and stopped in a cloud of dust near the porch, where the commander stood waiting.

Sidoron threw out his chest and tried to act the part of a dignified leader as he made his way to the back of the transport truck, but his hurried step gave him away. He barked an order and the tailgate was immediately lowered. A soldier grabbed a small, compact woman by the hair and dragged her out of the back of the truck.

Cody could see that she was young and that she was badly wounded. Her long brown hair was matted with dried blood. There was caked blood on her face. One arm hung limply by her side.

The commander asked her a question that Cody couldn't make out. Apparently he didn't like her answer. He backhanded the prisoner so hard she fell against the truck.

The woman didn't cry out. Instead she slowly rose and faced her attacker in silence. The commander barked another order and the soldiers pushed the prisoner up the steps to the interrogation room.

Cody untied the dirty red bandanna from around his forehead, shook his unkempt shoulder-length hair and wiped his grimy face with the back of his hand.

He thought about the woman. While he admired her spirit, he knew that it was only a matter of time until they broke her. He'd been in this camp for eighteen months, ever since Los Angeles had fallen in 2056, and he'd seen plenty of hard cases reduced to quivering idiots before the CCR—the

Confederation of Consolidated Republics—
was through.

Still, he'd made it his business to stay on
top of things and he wondered what it was
about this particular woman that had them all
so excited.

"Don't get too curious, kid. These guys
don't play around."

Cody shifted his gaze. Luther Swift was carrying a bucket filled with human excrement
in each hand. It was his job to dump the
makeshift toilets used in the barracks every
morning and evening. In between he dug
temporary latrines and covered them up again
when they were full.

Luther was a nuclear scientist. He had been
a fairly handsome man until the CCR gouged
out his right eye because he refused to reveal
the location of a nuclear research laboratory.
In the end they got their information.

"You know me, Luther," Cody said, trying
not to move his lips too much. "I mind my
own business."

It was against the rules for prisoners to talk
to each other, so Luther walked on. Quietly

he muttered, "See to it that you keep it that way. I don't much feel like picking up your pieces today."

Cody started hoeing again. He thought about his life in the old days before the takeover and wondered if there was anyone he knew still alive on the outside.

The CCR had control of more than three-fourths of the United States and its members considered themselves intellectually and physically superior to all Americans. After all, it was their stockpile of nuclear and chemical weapons that made all this possible. By concentrating their efforts into misleading the people of the United States into believing that their motives were harmless, the CCR had been able to buy property and plant spies in strategic places until everything was ready for the takeover.

The first missile took out Washington, D.C., and most of Virginia. The President, Congress and the Pentagon simply ceased to exist. Without leadership, the states began to panic and one by one to fall.

The United States government had made

it easy for them. Years before, the military had been cut back to a mere skeleton of what it had been during the cold war and the CIA had practically been disbanded. Never in their wildest dreams had the country's leaders considered the newly formed nation of the CCR a threat.

Bombings and mass murder had wiped out whole cities. Except for small rebel holdouts, the CCR had succeeded in reducing the citizens of what used to be the most powerful nation in the world to little more than slaves of the new republic.

Sidoron's prison camp was not unlike hundreds of others across the nation. There were twenty barracks inside the compound. One housed the commander's office and special quarters. The cooks, medical personnel and laundry were behind the office. Two buildings were for the guards, and the rest held prisoners.

Most of the inmates were civilians like Luther whom the CCR had left alive because they might have something valuable to contribute to the new world order. Others had been allowed to live to serve as laborers for the cause, but they never seemed to last long The soldiers were permitted to shoot and torture them at their own discretion.

Then there were the children. One whole barracks was devoted to American children of all races. Not that they didn't shoot children too. But a few of the lucky ones were involved in a cleansing experiment much like the one Hitler had tried with the youth of Germany. They had been taken from their parents and forced to attend daily classes designed to brainwash them into the correct attitude about the new government.

Cody was the oldest member of this last group. The enemy considered him one of their finest pupils. He could speak their language and spout their doctrine as well as anyone. And he went out of his way to convince them that he was completely loyal. No one knew what he was really up to, except Luther.

Cody's father had been a pilot in the third Gulf War—the conflict that had kicked off the endless string of wars. The Nighthawk F-119 he had flown had been shot down over what once had been called Iraq, and Cody had never heard from him again.

Cody's mother had been killed during the initial bombing attack on California, and until Cody had been captured he'd lived alone. Well, not entirely alone. There was Franklin Stubbs.

Franklin Stubbs had walked away from a maximum-security prison when it was hit by one of the bombs. At the time he had been serving five years for burglary. Since it was a well-known fact that the CCR exterminated all civil prisoners, he thought it best to leave when he had the chance.

A master safecracker and locksmith, Franklin spent his free time, when they weren't scavenging for food, teaching Cody the tricks of his trade. Cody returned the favor by allowing him to share his home, an out-of-the-way spot under a small bridge.

By day they slept to avoid patrols and at night they went into the burned-out city and searched for food. In the early-morning hours when it was light enough, Cody practiced his newfound vocation. Before long he knew how to make a lockpick out of almost anything and there wasn't a locked room or building anywhere that could keep him out.

But that was before. Before he and Franklin had had a run-in with a CCR foot soldier looking for military holdouts. The soldier shot first and asked questions later.

Franklin was left in a pool of blood and Cody was put on a transport plane heading for a prison camp in the southwest.

The memories made Cody set his jaw. Those things had happened more than a year ago. Since that time, he'd learned a lot, learned how to play their game. The guards trusted him now and had practically given him the run of the camp—which was exactly what Cody wanted.

CHAPTER 2

Deftly balancing a stack of clean white towels on one hand, Cody opened the front door with the other. He whistled as he passed the two guards stationed in front of Sidoron's private office. They paid no attention to him. He always seemed to be hanging around. It was his job to clean the office, deliver the laundry and bring the commander his evening meal.

Colonel Sidoron was sitting behind his desk puffing on an expensive cigar. When he noticed Cody, his face broke into a relaxed grin "And how is our little White Fox today?" he asked in accented English.

The teacher in Cody's new world order history class had first given him that nickname because of his ability to learn quickly and because of his white-blond hair. The camp guards had picked it up and now it was the only name they used for him.

Cody bowed the way he had been taught to do when addressed by a superior. Then, in the commander's own language, Cody assured him that things couldn't be better. He lowered his eyes and asked if there was anything His Excellency the colonel desired.

The colonel stood up and stretched. "No. You may clean my office now. I have something important to attend to."

And I bet I know who she is, Cody thought. He bowed again and waited for the colonel to leave the room. Pretending to put the towels away, Cody moved to a window and looked out through the half-open blinds.

"Just what I thought," he said under his breath. He watched the colonel and two guards walk straight to the isolation cells behind the office. These were metal boxes buried in the ground with only an iron grate for a roof. The sun, rain, dust and rats had easy access to them. Prisoners were sent there for punishment and most never left alive.

The colonel yelled down into one of the boxes, then spat on the prisoner below. The guards opened the padlock, pulled the grate off and lifted the woman out.

Cody drew a sharp breath. The woman's face was a mass of bruises, swollen to twice its normal size. Her broken arm had been twisted so that it now hung behind her at a crooked angle.

One of the guards pushed her with the barrel of his rifle and ordered her to walk ahead of him to the interrogation room. She took one step and fell. Instead of helping her up, the guards began kicking her in the stomach and ribs.

Cody clenched his fists and turned from the window. It wouldn't do either one of them any good for him to watch this. He would just do what he'd come here for and leave.

Quickly he put his towels on the shelf and moved to the colonel's desk. What he was looking for wasn't on it. He stepped to the file cabinet. From his pocket he took his latest pick wire, put it in the tiny lock and easily opened it.

He had already searched this cabinet several times, so it was a snap for him to recognize the new folder. The tab had the name McLaughlin printed on it in large block letters.

Cody thumbed through it. The woman was a pilot. Major Toni McLaughlin, formerly of the United States Air Force and lately of the U.S. Army Rebels. She had been shot down in a Blackhawk III chopper not far from the camp.

Cody rubbed his chin. Now, this was something. He had been told that the American holdouts were few in number and that they had no military capability. Apparently he'd been lied to. If the rebels had planes, they must have a base. And if McLaughlin knew where the base was located . . .

A door opened down the hall. Cody

slipped the file back into the cabinet and pushed the drawer shut. He picked up a feather duster and moved to the windowsill.

A young guard stuck his head in the office door. "Oh, it's only you, White Fox. You may carry on."

Cody bowed and managed a fake smile. Don't worry, sucker, he thought. I'll carry on, with or without your permission.

CHAPTER 3

It was dark but it didn't matter because the perimeter of the compound was well lit and a searchlight swept the area at regular intervals. The guards in the towers paced back and forth with their submachine guns watching for anyone who was careless enough to get caught in the firing zone.

Cody was squatting on the soles of his feet outside the commander's office waiting for Sidoron to finish his meal. One of the labor inmates had taught him a magic trick and he was showing it to the guards. First he tossed a shiny button in the air. Then he let them examine it. When they returned it he rubbed his hands together and . . . *poof*, it disappeared. The guards clapped and asked him to do it again.

He was about to make it vanish a second time when Sidoron called for him. Cody jumped to his feet and went into the office to retrieve the evening dishes.

The commander lit one of his smelly cigars and put his feet up on the desk. He watched Cody as he cleaned up what was left of the meal. "It is so hard to understand you Americans."

Cody didn't answer because the man seemed to be talking more to himself than anyone else.

Sidoron continued. "In the old days, it was easy to make people talk. Take away the food and water, maybe a few beatings. If necessary, shoot one of the relatives. My grandfather was an interrogator," he added proudly. "There was never a prisoner he could not make confess." He dropped his feet to the floor and sat up. "What is this foolish patriotism you Americans possess? Why would you be willing to be tortured?"

This time he was addressing Cody so the boy stopped gathering dishes onto the tray. "I'm sorry, Your Excellency, I don't know what you mean."

The commander sighed and leaned back in his squeaky chair. "Never mind, White Fox. You have become like us. I think perhaps you would not understand after all. Don't worry, it is not an insurmountable problem for me. I will look on it as a challenge."

Cody knew that Major McLaughlin was the problem Sidoron was talking about but also knew it would not serve his purpose to give that fact away. Instead he pretended to cheerfully pick up the tray and bowed his way out of the room.

Tonight Sidoron had left on his plate half a piece of white bread and a long strip of fat from his rare roast beef. Usually Cody would have gobbled it up the second he was out of sight. Compared to the watery porridge the inmates were served, anything tasted good. But tonight he had a plan for the leftovers.

He nodded at the guards and carried the tray out the side door. Wadding up the fat inside the bread, he held it in his hand until he was a few yards from the punishment cells. Quickly he tossed it at *her* box and kept walking.

When he was almost to the steps of the kitchen, he could have sworn he heard a whispered "Thank you" from inside the box.

He smiled.

CHAPTER 4

There were no adults in the children's barracks. The CCR didn't want them around to contaminate the younger inmates with poisonous American philosophies. Three times during the night a guard would make an inspection of the area. Everyone had to be on their bunk and no talking was allowed.

Cody was considered the ruler of this barracks. The other kids came to him to settle disputes and to discuss their problems. His cot was the only semiprivate one in the whole room. He had an entire corner to himself. Sometimes at night before the guard came he would entertain the rest of them by telling them about movies he'd seen or books he'd read. He even taught them a ball game they could play sitting on their bunks using a roll of wadded rags.

Tonight, though, he had made it clear that he wanted to be left alone. He had work to do. For the past six months he'd been working on a plan to escape. The biggest problem was that he had no idea where he was or what he would escape to. But now that problem was taken care of.

The instant he had read her file, he'd decided that the major was the key. She would know what lay on the outside and where the American rebels were hiding.

The lock on her punishment cell would pose no real obstacle. The padlocks all over the camp were the same brand. He had already opened several of them just to stay in practice. But getting her across the compound to his and Luther's escape route would take a little planning.

Luther. That brought up a new problem. What would he think about bringing the major along? They had worked out an escape for only two people. One more, a possible invalid at that, might endanger the whole thing.

The doorknob at the far end of the barracks turned. A tall guard with a gun slung over one shoulder marched in. He walked down the center aisle silently marking off the prisoners, making sure everyone was accounted for.

Cody stretched out on the hard bed and watched the man under half-closed eyelids. This guard was no different from the rest. They all assumed that the inmates of the children's barracks were not much of a threat so they never bothered to search them. Cody thought about the wire he had hidden inside his cotton mattress, which he used to make lockpicks. And carefully tacked to the underside of his board mattress was a full CCR uniform, his latest acquisition.

The guard left and Cody felt a tug on his left sleeve. It was Tasha, a five-year-old girl who had been brought in only three days ago. A large tear rolled down her cheek.

Cody wiped it away, sat up and lifted her onto the bunk beside him. "Hey, cut that out. I told you, you have to be brave in here."

Another tear escaped. "I been trying, Cody. Really. But I miss my mommy so bad. When do you think she's comin' for me?"

Cody sighed and put his arm around her small shoulders. "Sometimes it takes a while. You know how grown-ups are. They have a lot of business to take care of." He couldn't bring himself to tell her the truth. That her mom was probably lying dead somewhere with a CCR bullet between her eyes.

He gave Tasha a squeeze, carried her back to her bunk and pulled the threadbare, scratchy wool blanket over her. "Now, you stay in your bed. And try to get some sleep, okay?"

Minutes ticked into hours while Cody waited for the second inspection of the night. When the guard left, he quietly slipped off his cot and lifted a plank out of the wooden floor.

A grown man would have had trouble

squeezing through the small opening, but because of his age and the lack of nourishing food, Cody was able to slip through easily onto the ground under the barracks, carefully pulling the plank over the hole behind him.

He crawled to the corner of the barracks and waited for the searchlight to start moving in the opposite direction. When he was sure it was safe he ran to the next barracks and again waited for the light.

Luther's barracks was the third one down. Once more Cody ran through the darkness and waited. Then he ducked under the building and counted the floor joists as he felt his way along. When he reached the sixth one, he stopped. Quickly he tapped out a modified Morse code they had worked out, asking if Luther was listening.

In moments Luther's answer came back. No taps were wasted. Cody came right to the point. He told Luther about his plan to bring the woman. It was several seconds before Luther answered. It was simple—*no*.

Cody frowned. He tapped again, explaining that the major knew where the rebels were hiding. She could help them. Luther was adamant. They weren't taking the woman and that was final.

A scowl crossed Cody's face. He didn't have time to argue. The next inspection was coming up and he had something else he wanted to do before he went back to the barracks.

Swiftly he slid out from under the building and made his way across the yard. To be caught out in the open like this meant they would shoot him on sight. Cautiously he edged his way past the vegetable garden and stopped near a truck tire until the searchlight had scanned the area.

He took a deep breath and dropped to his stomach. Like a slow-moving snake he crawled across the dirt to the edge of the punishment cell.

"Psst. Major, are you there?"

There was no answer and the spotlight was sweeping back toward him. "Major?"

Silence.

Cody rolled into the shadows and stole back to his own barracks. Why hadn't she answered? Had they already beaten her so badly that she couldn't speak, or killed her?

He sat for a few seconds under his own barracks, listening before he moved the plank and slithered inside. There was barely time to hop onto his bunk before the door opened.

A bedbug was waiting for him. It bit him on the neck. He wanted desperately to swat it but since he was supposed to be asleep he had no choice but to endure it and wait.

His eyes traveled to the floor. In the dim moonlight he could see that he had put the plank back crooked. If the guard saw it, he would be sent immediately to the severe-punishment cell.

Cody reached down with his left hand. The plank was too far away. The guard was halfway down the barracks, counting.

"Please, mister, I gotta go."

Cody raised his head enough so that he could see who was talking. It was Tasha. She was standing on the end of her bed, sucking her thumb.

The guard pointed the glaring flashlight at

the little girl and shoved her. Tasha started wailing. Cody slid his foot out and adjusted the plank. Then he sat up. "Excuse me, Your Excellency, permission to speak."

The frustrated guard nodded his head. "Speak."

"The little girl just got here a couple of days ago and hasn't learned the rules yet. She's only five."

The guard was torn. If he disobeyed the camp regulations, he could be shot. He stiffened. "Teach her immediately, White Fox, or she will be terminated and replaced."

"Yes, Your Excellency." Cody bowed to the guard and then looked at Tasha sternly. "Go to sleep right now. I'll take care of everything. Just do what I say."

Tasha, still upset, slid under her blanket and buried her head.

The guard quickly counted the rest of the prisoners and left. Cody slipped off his cot and took Tasha to the waste bucket. He tried to explain to the tired girl that something very bad would happen to her if she didn't follow the rules.

He tucked her into bed for the second time. "Don't worry, Tasha, everything will be all right." To himself he muttered, "Because someday I'll get out of here and bring the whole U.S. Army back."

CHAPTER 5

School was held in one end of the laundry barracks. Classes weren't like any Cody had ever attended before. There were no desks or chairs. The students had to stand and listen while the instructor delivered the same lectures over and over, and no one was allowed to ask questions. If anyone got out of line, the guard stationed in the room took a thin iron rod and smacked them soundly on the back of the legs.

Today the teacher was discussing the loathsome, corrupt Americans and how they had lost their country because they were lazy and didn't deserve to have it in the first place. None of this ever made much sense to Cody. But he stored it away in the back of his mind just in case the instructor called on him to spew it back to her.

A small redheaded boy reached down to scratch one of his many bug bites. The guard picked up the rod and the boy immediately straightened and gave the teacher his full attention.

When the two-hour indoctrination class was over, the students were dismissed to have their breakfast and go to their workstations. Cody drank his lukewarm porridge and walked across the compound to the vegetable garden.

He took the faded red rag out of his pocket, rolled it up, tied it around his forehead and picked up the hoe. His shoulders slumped. His brief plan to include the major was over. Maybe it was for the best. The tunnel was probably only big enough for the two of them anyway.

Giving Luther the job of dumping the
waste buckets and digging the sewers was supposed to have been demoralizing, a way for
the CCR to show him who was really in
charge. But Luther saw it as an opportunity.
Instead of digging straight down, occasionally
he dug to the side closest to the fence. At the
end of the day he put just enough sand back
in the opening to fool the guards. They never
wanted to go down into the sewer pit and
look because of the smell.

Cody and Luther had made friends almost
from the start. Luther was wise enough to see
that Cody had some special talents that
might come in handy, one of which was his
ability to speak the Republic language. So he
invited Cody to come with him.

Cody had already been working on a few
schemes of his own. But Luther's was by far
the best. When he gave the signal, Cody was
to drop everything and meet him at the sewer.
The uniform under his cot was for Luther.
Luther spoke just enough of the Republic language so that if they were stopped they could
pretend that Luther was a CCR soldier who

had just captured the boy and was taking him to one of the camps.

Luther walked by the garden area carrying two of the buckets. He whispered, "I hear from the telegraph she's in the medical ward."

"The major?"

Luther gave a quick nod and moved on.

Cody hoed a little faster. The telegraph was a communications system the adult prisoners used between their barracks. It was hardly ever wrong. But this time it didn't make sense. Why would the CCR torture her and then try to fix her up?

A large weed had sprouted in the cauliflower section. Cody chopped at it thoughtfully. When he delivered the prison laundry this afternoon, maybe he'd get the chance to find out.

CHAPTER 6

The medical personnel weren't like the rest of the CCR. Most of them had been drafted to meet the growing needs in the new country. They resented being stuck in a prison camp and it showed in their crisp businesslike manner.

Cody pushed a metal cart across the hospital floor. It was stacked high with clean sheets, hospital gowns and towels. He stopped in front of the linen closet. It was locked.

Everything was kept under lock due to the amount of "borrowing" that went on among the soldiers.

He could have opened the lock himself but it would have given him away, so he pretended to search for an orderly.

Leaving the cart, he walked boldly into the next room. It was a ward with a row of beds along each wall. Most of the beds were full. Dysentery and flu were the biggest problems in the camp right now.

A nurse near the end bed was taking a soldier's temperature. "White Fox, you know you're not allowed in here. What are you doing?"

Cody bowed and scratched the back of his neck, trying to look as innocent as possible. "I brought the laundry cart and need to get in the linen cabinet."

"Go wait in the other room. I'll send someone." The nurse turned her back on him and attended to her patient.

Cody bowed again and deliberately went out the wrong door. He found himself in

another ward. This one had only a single
patient, and a makeshift curtain had been
drawn around the bed.

He edged closer to get a better look. The
patient was moaning deliriously—in English.

Cody's heart raced when he thought of
what would happen if he was caught in this
room. But he had to make sure. He pulled the
curtain back.

The major had a bandage wrapped around
her head and she was tossing and turning.
The doctor had set her dangling arm in a cast.
The other arm was solid purple with bruises.

"Major," Cody whispered urgently. "I am
an American. I want to help you. Can you
hear me?"

The moaning continued but the tossing
stopped. She turned her head and looked di-
rectly at him. She started blinking. It took
him a few moments to realize she was trying
to blink out words using Morse code.

*No give base location. Am acting crazy. Don't
know how much longer can fake . . .*

Cody leaned down and whispered in her
ear, "Hang in there, Major. And stay ready for

anything. I'm gonna try and get you out. Can you walk?"

"Yes," she blinked. A feeble smile made its way to her cracked lips. *"Thank God, marines are here."*

CHAPTER 7

When it came he wasn't expecting it. The adult telegraph passed him a strange message. A tall bald man with broken glasses was working the night shift peeling potatoes in the kitchen when Cody brought the colonel's evening tray in.

The man was whistling a silly tune and every so often he put some words to it. "Dum de dum, is tomorrow only a day away, dee de dum."

Cody almost dropped the tray. Was Luther

trying to tell him that after all these months the tunnel was finally ready?

He whirled around and raced out the kitchen door. If it was true, he had a busy night ahead of him. First on the list was to convince Luther that the major had to come with them.

The compound was quiet. It was almost time for bed check. He trotted up to the barracks door and pushed it open.

He stopped.

Something was wrong. The kids weren't in their beds. They were lined up, standing at attention at the far end. Soldiers were turning over bunks and knocking them to the floor.

A large hand grabbed his collar and flung him into the room. He skidded across the floor and landed on his back, looking up at Sidoron himself.

The commander knelt down and pinched Cody's jaws between his strong fingers. "So, you are loyal to the cause, eh, White Fox? You are one of us, right?" The man let go and slapped the boy on both cheeks. He stood and walked to the corner where Cody slept. With a swift kick he knocked the cot over.

The wire clattered to the floor and the uniform came loose from one of its tacks. Sidoron bent down and picked up a long strand of the smooth wire. He folded it and smacked it in the palm of his hand. "What is the meaning of this? What do you plan to do with it?"

Cody swallowed. He stood and shakily bowed. "There is no meaning, Your Excellency. I just sort of . . . collect things. It's an old American habit that's been hard for me to break."

"Liar." The colonel struck him across the face with the wire. "You are planning to escape. Who is the dog helping you?"

"N-No one, Your Excellency."

Sidoron used the wire on him again. "You will tell us. What is his name?"

Cody didn't answer.

"Take him to the punishment cell. Tomorrow he will talk—or he will die."

CHAPTER 8

Nights turned cold in the desert. Cody shivered in the bottom of the small square cell as he thought about this new turn of events. The future looked bleak. Tomorrow Sidoron would torture him until he told about Luther. If he didn't tell, they would kill him. In fact, they would probably kill him even if he did tell. The CCR wouldn't want him around as a reminder that their indoctrination program had been a failure.

He stood in one spot and rubbed his shoulders, trying to generate a little warmth. Sitting down was out of the question because the floor of the punishment cell was covered with human waste from the countless other prisoners who had been there before him.

The difference between the others and Cody was that he could get out of the cell anytime he wanted. In their rush to confine him, the guards hadn't bothered with a search, so he still had his homemade lockpicks.

But what if he did get out? Where would he go? They would find him anywhere he tried to hide inside the camp.

Using the tunnel wasn't a possibility. He couldn't ruin Luther's chance for escape just because he had been the one unlucky enough to get caught.

Ideas swam around in his head for hours. But there seemed to be no solution. The sun was already rising and he could hear the familiar noises of the camp beginning another day.

Breakfast passed him by, and then lunch. His stomach was growling and he was actually beginning to miss the watery, lukewarm porridge they served the prisoners between growing seasons.

By midafternoon the sun was beating down on him through the iron bars. He tied the rag around his head to keep the sweat from rolling into his eyes.

Finally they came for him.

The lock opened and the iron grate was pulled back. Cody squinted up at them. The two guards he'd shown the magic trick to the day before were standing above him. One of them reached down, grabbed Cody by the arm and dragged him out.

"Hey, guys, this is all a big mistake, I was only—"

A rifle butt smashed against the side of his head, knocking him to the ground. "The prisoner will not speak."

Cody shook his head to clear his vision and managed to struggle to his knees before the second guard caught him in the ribs with the steel toe of his army boot.

Knowing that he shouldn't just lie there and make himself an easy target for them, he rolled and then jumped to his feet. Blood trickled down the side of his face and his ribs ached like fire but he did his best not to let the pain show.

The guards pushed him up the steps and inside the building. The interrogation room was at the end of the long hall. He'd never been inside before but he'd heard the screams of the prisoners who had.

Sidoron was waiting for him, seated behind a large wooden desk in the middle of the room. The guards shoved him forward to a small metal chair in front of the desk.

After standing all night and most of the day, he was glad to sit down. Sidoron lit up one of his cigars and walked around the desk. He carefully looked Cody up and down and then sat on the edge of the desk with his arms folded.

"You've been with us a long time, White Fox, eh?"

Cody nodded.

"During this time you have probably come to know a lot of the other prisoners. Corrupt men who would use a bright boy like you to get what they wanted for themselves."

Cody stared at the desktop while the commander continued. A long silver needle attached to a syringe caught his attention. He shifted his gaze and tried not to think about it.

"You're young and don't understand the mind-set of these types of people. They aren't really your friends, you know. They're only using you. If you were to turn them in, you would be perfectly justified. No one would hold it against you."

Cody swallowed and bowed from the waist. "Your Excellency, you don't understand. It was all a joke. I was going to return the uniform. And I was using the wire to make toys for the children in the barracks. What reason would I have to lie to you?"

The man stood. His pockmarked face was contorted with an evil grin. "So you are saying that you are happy here? You are completely loyal to our cause?"

The boy nodded again, not daring to look up.

"I wonder if you would care to prove it? See the dirt on my boots? Do you think it is becoming for a man of my importance to have such grime on himself? Of course you don't. Get it off."

Cody dropped to the floor and started to use his hand to wipe one of the black boots.

"No, White Fox. I want you to lick it off."

Cody looked at the boot. A voice in his head said, *Go ahead, maybe he'll believe you and let you off. . . .*

But his body refused to obey. His back stiffened and he moved to the chair to wait for the inevitable.

"Just as I thought." Sidoron rubbed his hands together. "Now we can stop the games. You were planning to escape. And one or more of the adults are involved in this plot. I want to know their names. You will tell me who they are, or what's left of you won't be enough to feed the rats."

"There was no one else," Cody insisted desperately. "I was going out by myself."

"Really?" The commander took the long cigar out of his mouth and turned the smoldering end toward Cody's arm. "Are you sure there was no one?" He pushed it slowly into the boy's flesh.

Cody jumped sideways, knocking the chair over. Sidoron motioned for the guards. They held Cody down on the floor while the commander burned him again and again on his arms and chest.

He could not stop the scream, a high-pitched keening sound that seemed to come from somewhere else, someone else.

"Put him back in the chair," Sidoron barked. "Perhaps he is ready to talk now."

Cody was in agony. And he knew this was only the beginning.

Sidoron slapped his face. "Pay attention, boy. Who are your accomplices?"

"I . . . I was going alone."

A large hard-rubber club about the length of Sidoron's forearm was lying on the desk. He picked it up and again motioned for the guards to hold the boy.

CHAPTER 9

When they threw him back in the cell, Cody landed on the bottom with a thud. He lay on the filthy floor too hurt and tired to move. Sidoron had beaten every inch of his body. Then the guards had had their fun. His shirt was ripped and he was bleeding all over.

Tomorrow would be worse.

The flies swarmed around his cuts. He didn't even try to wave them away. Maybe Sidoron would go ahead and kill him tomorrow and it would be over. He closed his eyes, wishing that somehow he could make it all go away.

Sleep wouldn't come. His mind would not stop hoping for some kind of relief.

Comfort did come. It was in the form of another song. A guard escorted an adult prisoner who had pulled night duty in the kitchen past the punishment cells. Suddenly the man burst out singing. "'When the moon is high, my baby and I are leaving this one-horse town.'"

The guard yelled at the man to be quiet and punched him between the shoulder blades with the barrel of his rifle. The prisoner coughed and staggered across the compound to his barracks.

"Good old Luther." Cody looked above him through the bars of the iron grate. The camp was quiet and the moon was on its way up.

There was no time to lose.

With gritted teeth and superhuman effort he rolled over and forced himself to his feet. The cell started spinning. He reached for the wall to steady himself. He felt as if he needed to vomit, only there was nothing in his stomach. Cody chided himself. "Come on, Pierce . . ."

It took a few seconds for the throbbing in his head to clear. Ignoring the pain shooting through his body, he drew his best lockpick out of his pants and reached through the bars to the padlock.

It made a creaking noise when it snapped open. Cody dropped the lock and the pick into his shirt pocket, pushed up on the grate and forced himself to climb out.

Immediately he made for the cover of the shadows near the office. There was only one thought on his mind—the major—and he knew Luther wasn't going to like it. Cody had promised her he would try to do something to get her out and now he had to keep his word. Besides, they would need her to help find the base.

His heart was pounding as he silently crept toward the back of the medical barracks. He tried the first window. It was nailed shut. So were the second and third. The wood on the fourth window had swollen from the last rain so that it stuck. After dodging the searchlight several times, he finally managed to open it wide enough to squeeze through.

He landed on a bruised shoulder in the operating room. A dim light shone in from the adjoining ward. From the cover of the surgical cabinet, he could see a duty nurse making her rounds.

When she finished, Cody crawled past the cabinet into the ward. He crossed his fingers, hoping that the patients were either asleep or too sick to notice him.

He was almost to the next door when something behind him crashed to the floor. Cody slid under one of the beds.

The duty nurse came rushing back. Cody could only see her feet and they were running straight to the bed next to his.

"Private Rykov, I've told you a thousand times not to get out of bed by yourself. Here, let me help you."

Cody waited, fearing that the rapid beating of his heart or his loud breathing would give him away.

The nurse helped the young man down the ward to the bathroom. The instant they were out the door, Cody moved out from under the bed and hurried into the next room.

The major was still there.

Wasting no time, he went to her bed and gently shook her awake. Her eyes flew open. She didn't hesitate or ask for an explanation. Quietly she slid off the bed, grabbed what was left of her flight suit and boots from the closet and followed him on her battered hands and knees across the ward floor.

CHAPTER 10

Cody held his hand up. The major stopped behind him and waited. From the shadows near the office he could see several sets of headlights approaching the camp.

Three small units and two official-looking black cars with flags on the hoods pulled into the compound. Cody had seen cars like these and men like the ones stepping out of them before.

It was a surprise inspection. Sidoron's superiors came several times a year to make sure everything was in order. This time they would be especially interested in two things. One would be how the indoctrination program was working and the other—Cody glanced back at the major—was hiding with him here in the bushes.

Lights started coming on in the headquarters and the guardhouse. Cody looked at the moon. It wasn't quite up all the way.

They couldn't stay where they were. There was no choice but to head for the sewer pit.

The major stayed right behind him. When he jumped into the pit, she didn't falter. He went to work frantically, clearing the tunnel entrance. Without a word the major slipped into her boots and used her good arm to help.

When the opening was clear, Cody went to the edge of the smelly pit and peeked out. If Luther didn't get here soon, they'd be forced to leave without him.

A furtive movement caught his eye at the side of the toolshed. Cody ducked so that whoever was out there wouldn't see him. Then he heard a noise like someone crawling in the dirt on their belly.

Luther dropped quietly into the pit beside him. "We got big trouble, kid. We'd be better off to try for another night. The whole place is crawling with . . ." He saw the major still in her hospital gown kneeling near the tunnel entrance. Luther rubbed his chin and paused. "Just tell me one thing. Has she given them the location of the base?"

Cody shook his head.

Luther threw up his hands. "Then what are we waiting for? Let's get out of here." He took a small spade out of his belt and darted into the tunnel.

Cody and the major followed. Luther had done an excellent job of digging. The tunnel was deep and it went out under the wire for a good twenty feet. Now all he had to do was punch out an opening through the topsoil.

Dirt fell on them as Luther dug but no one talked. In a few minutes he had a hole wide enough to crawl through.

An alarm went off.

They could hear shouting and people running.

Luther crawled over the major and grabbed

Cody's shoulders. "Listen to me and don't argue. You were right to bring the major. We can't let them have her information. Now it's going to be your job to help her get away. I'm going back to draw their attention. It'll take their minds off of her for a while and buy you some time."

"Wait." Cody grabbed at Luther's foot but he was already halfway back to the pit.

"Go on," Luther whispered. "If I'm going to play the hero, I don't want it to be wasted."

Numbly Cody followed the major down the tunnel to the opening and helped her out. Then he squirmed up behind her and started running.

They could hear more shouting. In moments the sound of machine-gun fire came from the camp. Cody turned. The spotlights were focused on the fence and he could see the outline of Luther's lifeless body hanging from the top of the barbed wire.

Cody felt a hand slide inside his own and pull him along. "Come on, kid. He didn't die so that we could stand around. We need to keep moving."

CHAPTER 11

Running was torture. At first the adrenaline pumping through his veins kept him moving. He was too scared not to. But now his legs ached from the beating he had received earlier and he could feel himself slowing down.

They had been traveling fast for hours. It had been Cody's idea to drop off into a canyon bed for cover and see where it took them.

Twice helicopters had flown over using searchlights but the two escapees had plastered themselves to the wall of the canyon and the helicopters had flown on.

Cody slowed to a walk. The major fell into step beside him. "You look pretty rough, kid. What did they want from you?"

He shrugged. "Somehow they found out I was planning to escape. They wanted me to give them my partner's name and I wouldn't." A picture of Luther hanging from the fence crowded into his mind.

The major touched his arm. "He was a very brave man."

Cody moved into a slow trot. He didn't want to talk about it. If he hadn't brought the woman . . . the thought trailed off.

He glanced back at her. She was small, not even as tall as him. Her face was still bruised but starting to look a little better. He had to give her credit. She'd taken a lot from Sidoron and had still managed to survive. The bandage on her head and the cast on her right arm were filthy from the dirt in the tunnel and from sliding down the canyon bank.

She had changed into the olive green flight suit the CCR had found her in. Both sleeves had been ripped off and it was torn in a couple of other places. Grudgingly he admitted to himself that she had kept up with him in spite of her injuries.

They trudged on through the morning and into the afternoon. A trickle of water had emerged on the base rock of the canyon floor. Cody dropped to his knees to get a drink. The major did the same.

He watched her. She held her bad arm in the air and tried to sip the water while lying on her left shoulder.

"Can I help you?" he heard himself asking.

The major sat up and wiped her mouth. "No thanks. I'll manage."

Cody looked at the sky. The sun was high. The CCR was probably scouring the countryside by now. He hoped they would search the roads and towns before they looked for them in the desert.

His stomach made a loud growling noise, reminding him that he'd missed several meals. "How far is the base, Major?"

She pursed her lips. "Clear across the state. We won't be able to walk it. Sooner or later we're going to need some kind of transportation. And by the way, the name is Toni. What's yours?"

"Cody. Cody Pierce."

Toni put out her left hand. "Glad to meet you, Cody. And thanks for getting me out of that place."

Shyly Cody shook her hand. "No problem. I just hope our getting out was worth what it cost."

CHAPTER 12

It was getting too dark to see. Cody found an overhang on the canyon wall and made the decision to stop for the night. When he was younger, his father had taught him some basic survival skills, so he knew how to make a fire, but he decided it was far too risky.

Using his wire lockpick, Cody stabbed some of the red fruit on a large cactus and gave part of it to Toni. Earlier, when they'd been by the water, he had picked some cattails and other roots. He took them out of his shirt and gave her some. "I know it's not the best . . ."

Toni took it all gratefully. "After that runny oatmeal at the prison camp, I bet it tastes just fine."

They ate in silence, barely able to see each other's face. Cody wiped his hands on his pants. "How big is the base?"

"Big enough. Listen, it might be better if I don't give you any details until we're sure there's no danger of the CCR catching up with us."

Cody was angry. He knew she was right but all this was incredible news to him and he wanted to know more. "Couldn't you at least tell me how our side is doing?"

Toni chose her words carefully. "Let's just say we have gained some powerful allies. I was on my way back to the base with some information that could change everything. Now, can we talk about something else?"

"Like what?"

"Like you. How old are you?"

"Almost fifteen."

"You have any family?"

"Nope. The CCR took care of that. How about you?"

"I was married once. To another pilot. He was killed last year when they bombed Jennings Air Base in Nevada."

They lapsed into silence again. Cody thought about how young she looked to already be a widow. He yawned and leaned back. "I guess we better try and get some sleep. We'll have to start at first light."

"Tomorrow we're going to have to leave the canyon. It's starting to head in the wrong direction."

Cody sat up. "I don't want to be a pest or anything, but would it be a big deal for you to tell me which direction we should be going?"

"East toward the mountains . . . Cody?"

"Yeah?"

"If anything happens to me I want you to find a Colonel Wyman. Tell him . . . proceed with Dark Angel."

"Nothing is going to happen to you. We're going to get through."

Toni slid down and tried to get comfortable on the cold rock ledge. "I hope you're right."

CHAPTER 13

Cody's eyes flickered and opened. A pink sun was just coming up over the sandy horizon. He sat up and looked at Toni. She was still asleep, curled in a tiny ball.

He hated to wake her but it had to be done. Reaching across, he lightly touched her arm.

"*No. Not again.*" Her scream ripped through the morning air.

"It's okay, Toni." Cody shook her. "It's just me. You're safe."

Toni sat up. Her eyes were wild and she was shaking. It took a few seconds for her to realize where she was and calm down. "Bad dream . . ."

"I have them sometimes." Cody sat beside her, waiting. His own experience at Sidoron's hands had been awful. "I used to have them all the time but not so many now."

She put her hand to her forehead. "I'm . . . sorry, I . . ."

"You don't have to explain. I've been there, remember?" He stepped out into the canyon, stabbed several juicy pieces of fruit from a prickly pear and brought them to her. "Here. Better eat these. We need to get going."

"Right. Lead the way, I can eat as we go."

Cody found a place where ancient waters had carved a crevice in the wall of the canyon. He started climbing out and Toni scrambled up behind him.

They were in the open now with only greasewood and cactus for cover. In the distance Cody could see a piece of an old dirt trail. If they followed it, they might find the transportation they so badly needed. On the other hand, it would be easier for the enemy to spot them.

He decided to compromise. They would make for the trail but not get close enough to it that anyone checking it could see them.

As usual Toni followed without complaint. He picked up two small pebbles and handed her one. "Put this in your mouth and you won't get so thirsty." He broke into a trot. "Let me know when you get tired."

They moved across the gray dirt, putting the camp far behind them. Since Toni never said anything, Cody tried to keep an eye on her. When he thought she needed to rest, he stopped and crawled next to one of the bushes for what little shade it offered.

By the middle of the afternoon, the sun had become almost unbearable. Cody could feel his face and arms blistering. He slowed down and looked back. Toni didn't look too good. She was staggering as if she were drunk and her lips were a strange bluish color.

He ran back barely in time to catch her as she fell. Her skin felt dry, without a hint of perspiration. He put her down near a greasewood bush, pulled off his shirt and began fanning her with it.

Cody had seen cases of heatstroke at the prison camp. He knew she would die if he couldn't cool her down.

He laid her head on the sand, took the pebble out of her mouth and looked around. A barrel cactus was growing a few feet away. Using the piece of wire, he sawed at the top until it came off, scooped out some of the cool, slimy green insides and washed her face. Then he went back for more. This time he forced some of the bitter-tasting liquid into her mouth.

She swallowed but stared at him unblinking. Cody continued to smear the cold slime on her arms and neck. Her breathing seemed to return to normal but her skin still felt dry.

"Toni?" Cody fanned her while he talked. "I'm going up the trail now to look for water." He draped his shirt over the bush to produce a little more shade for her. "Don't die on me, okay?"

There was no response. Cody stood up, spotted the trail and started for it. He found it a well-beaten path used by animals. Fresh tracks headed in both directions.

The tracks gave Cody hope. If there were animals out here, they had to have water too. All he had to do was find it.

He topped over a low rise and stopped. Using his hand to shield his eyes, he scanned the sloping ground in front of him.

Something shiny caught his attention. The sun transformed whatever was out there into waves of hot rolling silver. As he moved closer, he could also make out the shape of a building.

He squinted to make sure his eyes weren't playing tricks. The silver thing was a water tank and standing beside it was a windmill, its blades lazily turning in the slight breeze.

"Yes!" Cody jumped into the air and raced back down the trail.

He found Toni lying where he'd left her, only now her eyes were closed. He dropped to his knees and listened for a pulse. She was still alive.

Even though she was slight, Cody knew he'd never be able to carry her all the way to the tank. So he stood at her head, reached under her arms and walked backward, dragging her toward the animal trail.

The sweltering sun was merciless and his progress seemed incredibly slow. Twice he tripped and once he fell, dropping Toni in the dirt. When he finally reached the rise, he sank to the ground for a short rest. His arms ached and his body yearned to stop. Willing himself to stand, he slowly reached down and took hold of her once more. One backward excruciating step at a time, he pulled her down the sandy incline.

He slogged along—it felt as if she gained a hundred pounds with each step—and just as he thought he could do no more he heard the sound of running water. He looked over his shoulder and saw it—crystal-clear water coming out of a small round pipe into a metal storage tank.

"We're almost there, Toni. Hang on." Cody pulled her to the edge of the tank, put his hand in the water and splashed it on her face. Then he picked her up, dropped her over the edge and jumped in after her.

It felt like heaven. He pushed her under and went down with her. Coming up from the second plunge, she coughed and her eyes fluttered open.

Her cast started to disintegrate and the bandage slipped off her head. Cody held on to her so that she wouldn't drown. "I told you we'd make it, Toni."

Something cracked behind him. Cody whirled around. A large blond woman in a faded housedress was standing a few feet away, pointing a shotgun at them.

In the Republic language she ordered, "You two stay right where you are. Move one inch and you're dead."

CHAPTER 14

"Where am I?" Toni lifted her head. She was wearing a large nightgown and resting on a stack of pillows in a feather bed with real sheets. The room was small and furnished with antiques from the seventies and eighties.

Something at the foot of the bed stirred. She rose up on her good arm to get a better look. It was Cody. He was stretched out, snoring softly on a colorful homemade rag rug.

Toni reached behind her for one of the pillows and tossed it at him. Cody woke with a start. "What the . . ." He sat up. "Oh, it's you," he said crossly. "It's about time you woke up. We have a lot of ground to cover."

"What happened? The last thing I remember was walking in the desert. How did we get here?"

The door opened and the stout blond woman from the water tank came in carrying a tray with glasses and sandwiches. "Good. You're awake." She set the tray down on the nightstand. "You must hurry now. Orlo will be back soon."

Toni looked confused. "Who's Orlo?"

Cody stood up and took one of the sandwiches. "Thank you, Anna. As soon as my sister is ready, we'll be on our way."

"That's good. I'll just go downstairs and make you something to take with you. Do try and hurry now," she repeated as she closed the door.

"That was Anna," Cody said between bites. "Here, have a sandwich." He held out the tray for her. Toni took one of the larger ones and Cody continued, "You tried to cut out on me back there in the desert. I barely got you here alive. Anna found us in her water tank. After I explained how we *broke down* out in the desert and had gotten ourselves lost looking for shelter, she was kind enough to help take care of you."

"How long have we been here?"

"All last night and most of today. Anna put that splint on your arm and doctored your head. But if you feel up to it she wants us to leave as soon as possible. She's American but her husband, Orlo, runs this satellite outpost for the CCR. She's expecting him back today."

Toni pulled back the sheet and tried to stand up. "Ohhh." She held her forehead.

Cody reached out to steady her. "Are you going to be okay?"

"Yeah, sure. Help me find my clothes."

"Your flight suit got kinda shredded on the way here. I had to drag you a pretty long way." He picked up a large plaid shirt and an equally large pair of red shorts. "Anna says you can have these."

Toni smiled. "I guess beggars can't be choosers. Wait for me downstairs. I'll just be a minute."

CHAPTER 15

Toni helped herself to a couple of the sandwiches and then cautiously made her way down the stairs. She had found a safety pin on the dresser and adjusted the shorts so that they wouldn't fall off. The shirt hung down to her knees but she rolled up the sleeves and made it work.

Cody was waiting for her at the kitchen table, eating cookies. When he saw Toni, he gulped his milk and put the glass in the sink.

"Looks like we're ready now, Anna. Thanks for everything. You've been a real lifesaver."

"I'd like to add my thanks too," Toni said. "Maybe someday we can return the favor."

"Just please don't tell anyone you were here. It is against the new law to help Americans." Anna handed Cody a paper sack. "There's food in here. Maybe it'll keep you for a while." She followed them to the screen door. "Stay on the road. It'll take you to Marsden. But be careful. There are plenty of soldiers there who would rather shoot than arrest you."

"We'll be careful. Thanks again."

They passed two buildings about a half mile down the road. The closest one looked like a barn but had a tower antenna on the top and a satellite dish near the front.

The second building was the one that interested Toni. It was taller and wider than the barn. A smooth dirt road led up to its large double doors.

She glanced back over her shoulder. The house was too far away for Anna to see them.

Toni pulled Cody to the side of the strange building.

"What are you doing?" he whispered. "Anna said there was no danger until Orlo gets back."

Toni faced him. "I want to get a look inside this building. It could be important."

"Why? I already checked about a truck. Orlo has the only one they own. We're just going to have to walk into that town she told us about and see what we can come up with."

"Maybe not." Toni moved around to the door, pulled it open a few inches and peeked in. "Take a look at this."

Cody was already looking over her shoulder. Parked inside was a small two-seater airplane in camouflage green. He folded his arms. "Well, what do you know? My dad would have loved this. I think they quit making those back in the early eighties. Think you can fly it?"

"Normally I'd brag and say I could fly anything. But because of this arm, you may have to help me a little. Are you willing?"

Cody chewed his lip. "It's not a very nice

thing to do to Anna after the way she helped us."

"Anna is an American. I don't want to make trouble for her any more than you do, but our primary mission here is to help our country."

"I guess you're right. Tell me what to do."

"Open those doors and let's get her outside."

CHAPTER 16

In the bright sunlight Toni was able to quickly examine the light airplane. It appeared to be flight-ready. She climbed up into the copilot's seat. Cody shut the door for her and ran around to the pilot's side.

She checked the instrument panel. The plane was old but all the basic navigational aids were there. The stick was new to her but with Cody's help they could probably manage. It had been her idea to sit on this side of the plane so that she could use her good arm for the center controls.

Cody shut his door and waited for instructions. Toni turned a knob and inspected the fuel gauge. The needle pointed to Full.

"Cross your fingers, Cody. If she starts, our takeoff may be a little rough. When I get going, I'm going to need you to help me with this stick, okay? Just pull back on it slowly. When we're up, I should be able to handle it. Ready?"

Cody gave her the thumbs-up sign. She started the engine. It coughed and sputtered, then settled into a smooth purr. Slowly the plane began moving down the dirt runway, the speed increasing as they neared the end.

"Okay, flaps are down. Let's get this baby up."

Together they pulled back on the control stick. The plane jumped, touched down and then jerked into the air.

They were flying.

Toni checked the instrument panel and leveled the plane out just a few hundred feet in the air. She glanced over at Cody. "I'm trying to keep it low so that radar won't pick us up. It's chancy, though, because we could be spotted from the ground."

Cody looked down at the desert floor. "All I know is, it sure beats the heck out of walking. How long will it take us to get there in this?"

"It's not the fastest thing I've ever flown, but if we're lucky, we should be there in a few hours."

For the first hour they hardly talked. Cody fell asleep with his head against the door. When he woke up, Toni began asking him questions about his life before prison and his family. "Did you ever fly with your dad?"

"Naw. He was supposed to teach me but he never got the chance."

"How about a quick lesson?"

"Now?"

"Why not? You might need to get out of a tough spot sometime. Besides, the army can always use more good pilots."

"In that case, start teaching."

"First let's take a look at some of the instruments." Toni went over the functions of the altimeter, speed indicator, horizon indicator and compasses. Then she quizzed him. He repeated almost word for word everything she'd told him.

"I'm impressed, Cody. You're a quick learner."

"I picked it up in prison. The faster I could learn stuff the better job they thought they were doing. They even gave me a nickname—White Fox."

"You're the White Fox? Now I'm really impressed. I heard some of the guards talk about you. You were supposed to be one of their finest success stories. Colonel Wyman is definitely going to want to meet you."

"I didn't do anything special. All I did was survive the best way I knew how."

"You saved my skin. I think that's kind of special."

Cody felt uncomfortable. "Can we get back to the lesson? We'll be at the base before you get around to letting me have the controls."

"The controls are the easy part. Here."
Toni put her good hand behind her head and
leaned back. "Take them."

Cody grabbed at the control stick and the
plane pitched upward.

"Don't be so rough," Toni scolded. "Hold it
gently and keep your eyes on the instruments.
Push it forward and the nose drops, back and
we go up."

Cody watched the panel carefully, almost
afraid to breathe. After a few minutes he relaxed. "Hey, this isn't so hard. It's almost
like—"

The plane lunged, making a choking
sound, and then the engine stopped. Toni sat
up. She tapped one of the gauges and it swung
violently to the left.

"What's wrong?" Cody demanded. "Did I
break something?"

"No. It's not your fault. Looks like we
might have a leak in the fuel line. We're
going down. Get ready."

Cody looked at the ground below. The
desert had changed to green landscape with
fields and a few trees. They had passed a small

town an hour or so earlier. He wondered if anyone would come out to help them—or, more likely, arrest them.

It all seemed like a dream. The plane was fighting them, trying to head straight down while he and Toni fought to keep its nose up.

Then abruptly the ground that had looked so far away rushed up to meet them. Trees sped by, snatching at the plane with their branches. With one bone-jarring crunch both wings were sheared off and the windshield blew out in pieces.

At high speed, the small aircraft skidded across a field and came to a grinding stop on the edge of an arroyo, its nose buried in a large bank of dirt.

CHAPTER 17

Out of the corner of his eye Cody could see his arms and hands. He raised his head. Nothing seemed to be broken. His forehead ached and he had several new cuts from the broken glass but he was still alive.

He turned to look at Toni. She was hunched over, holding her fractured arm. "This thing is never going to heal if I don't quit cracking up airplanes."

Cody smiled with relief. "You probably hold the record for the most crash landings in the shortest period of time." He unsnapped his seat belt. "Flying was sure nice while it lasted but I guess it's back to walking."

He was just about to try his door when it was yanked open. A burly farmer stabbed at him with a pitchfork. In the Republic language he ordered Cody to get out of the aircraft.

Another, younger man dressed in worn overalls, with arms as big around as tree trunks, held a small pistol. He waved it in the air victoriously. "We've captured some Americans, Papa. The CCR will reward us."

Cody put his hands up and slipped down out of the plane. He spoke to them in their language. "Don't shoot. My partner is hurt. Help us. We are on a secret mission for the CCR."

The two men put their heads together and whispered. The young one turned to Cody. "Where are your papers?"

"I told you, we're on a special mission. We don't carry papers."

The farmer pointed the pitchfork at the plane. "You are only a boy, too young to be flying planes. Get your partner out. We will talk to him."

They followed Cody around to Toni's door. He tried to open it but it was stuck. The young man with the muscular arms gave the pistol to his father and reached up to help. With one tug he wrenched it off its hinges.

Toni had heard them talking. She didn't understand the language but she figured Cody was doing his best to make up a cover for them. When they opened the door she was lying motionless on the controls with her eyes closed.

"See," Cody said. "I told you my partner was hurt."

The young man shrugged and picked her up as if she were a child and set her on the ground.

Again the two men conferred. Cody could hear snatches about how big the reward would be if he and Toni turned out to be spies.

Finally they made a decision. They would take the two fliers back to the farm and lock them in the root cellar until they notified the nearest CCR garrison.

The young man picked up Toni and started across the field. Cody had to trot to keep up with him. The older man stayed behind them, holding the gun.

As they approached the house, Cody scanned the area for signs of transportation. A rusty truck sat in front of the farmhouse with its hood up and two flat tires. The only other vehicle on the place was an old green tractor parked in the field.

The farmer unlocked the cellar and held the door open for his son. The young man dropped Toni on a stack of corn husks and turned to Cody. "If you are who you claim to be, you will be free to go in a few days. If you are not . . . well, I wouldn't want to be in your shoes when the soldiers get here." He grinned and pretended to slice his throat with his thumb. Laughing, he stepped out the door and locked it behind him.

Toni sat up. She waited until she heard footsteps moving away from the door. Then she spoke in a low voice. "Do you see any way out of here? The floor is made of dirt. Maybe we could dig our way out."

"Why don't we just go out the way we came in?" Cody took out his lockpick and felt for the keyhole. In seconds he had the door unlocked.

Toni put her hand on his shoulder. "Did anyone ever tell you that you are amazing?"

"Wait till you see my magic tricks." Cody pushed the door open a crack. "They must have gone in the house to make some calls. I don't see anybody."

"In that case, let's go. I don't think it's going to be too healthy for us to hang around here."

Cody slipped through the door, waited for Toni and then closed it. The old farmer had left his pitchfork leaning against the outside wall and when Cody turned he tripped on it, sending it clattering to the ground.

"Hey. What's going on there?" The son came running from the hay shed. He grabbed Cody by the collar and squeezed, nearly choking the life out of him. Toni jumped on the large man's back. He let go of Cody and pulled Toni over his head. She landed flat on her back with the wind knocked out of her.

Cody grabbed the pitchfork and jabbed with it threateningly. "Stay back. I won't hurt you if you leave us alone."

The big man laughed. "You think you can take me with that? You are nothing but a small puppy. I will make you eat it."

He faked left and lunged. Cody brought the pitchfork up in front of him, aiming at the man's legs, but the movement threw him off and the big man took the prongs full in the stomach. He dropped to one knee, his face white, staring at the fork in disbelief. "I've been killed . . . killed by a . . . boy."

Cody dropped the handle and stepped back. Toni made it to her feet. She pulled on his arm. "Come on. You did what you had to. There's no time to think about it."

Cody swallowed. The fork, he thought, the fork had just been there and then it had disappeared into the man's stomach. Just there and . . .

He shook his head and turned and blindly followed her toward the mountains.

CHAPTER 18

"Are you sure there's a base up here?"

Toni nodded. "I'm sure."

"Why would they put it in the mountains? Nobody would want an air base in the middle of a bunch of trees."

"That's what we're hoping the CCR will think. Just over this next hill is the Jicorrilla Valley. It's a perfect hiding spot, surrounded on all sides by the mountains."

Cody scrambled up the hill behind her.

He was breathing hard. "What do you say we take a break? This altitude is killing me."

At the top of the ridge, Toni dropped to her stomach and pointed below them. "See, I told you. There it is."

Cody frowned. "I don't see anything."

"Look carefully. Almost everything is covered with camouflage netting."

Cody knelt and studied the scenery. There were breaks in the trees and bushes where large green blobs sat. "I think I see it now. They've done a good job disguising it."

Toni turned to him. "Still want to take that break? Or would you like to meet part of the team that's going to get our country back?"

Cody stood. "Part of the team? You mean there are more?"

"We have three bases in strategic locations and there are ground troops just waiting for the order to fight. Also, Canada, Mexico and England have agreed to lend their support.

That's part of the information I was bringing back when I was shot down."

Cody started moving down the hill. "What are you doing standing around up here talking? We've got a war to fight."

Colonel Wyman was a tall man. His hair was almost silver and his eyes were bright blue. When he had finished debriefing Toni, he asked to see Cody.

Cody had eaten a large meal and then gone out exploring the base. He couldn't believe the number of guns, planes and missiles. When he had been captured, the CCR had told him that the United States military had been completely crushed and that the new Republic had absolute control.

He felt a tap on his shoulder. "Excuse me, sir, the colonel will see you now." A young sergeant led him to a large brown tent with open flaps.

Toni was just coming out. She looked around. "Well? What do you think?"

"You were right. It's great."

"I'm headed over to medical." She held up her arm. "Maybe this time I can get it put back together and keep it that way. When you get through talking to the colonel, come see me."

Cody nodded and followed the sergeant inside the tent. The colonel was seated at a table talking to his aide. When he saw Cody he rose and walked around the table to shake his hand. "Come in, young man. Major McLaughlin tells me you are responsible for helping her escape and for saving her life on several occasions."

"I guess we were lucky."

"Lucky?" The colonel laughed and turned to the aide. "Did you hear that, Jeff? The boy is modest."

The aide nodded. "Yes, sir. I'd say so."

Colonel Wyman indicated a chair. "Sit down, son. I've got a few questions to ask you."

Cody hesitated. The small chair in Sidoron's interrogation room flashed through his mind. He took a deep breath and forced himself to sit.

The colonel sat also. "I understand that you've been a prisoner for quite some time?"

"Yes, sir. Almost a year and a half."

"And during that time you learned to speak the Republic language fluently?"

"Yes, sir."

"Can you give us the details of how these camps are run? What is the general layout . . ."

The colonel asked questions for another hour about Cody's life as a prisoner while the aide took notes. A few times the colonel asked the same question in a different form. Cody knew it was to see if he would trip himself up or if he was really what he claimed to be.

Finally the colonel stood up. "Well, I guess that about covers it, son. We can't thank you enough for helping the major the way you did. She was carrying some vital information. You can be very proud of yourself."

Cody looked up at the tall man. "So what happens now?"

"Now I'll send for someone to escort you to

a tent where you can get some rest. You're probably worn out from your journey."

"And then what?"

The colonel scratched his head. "Then we'll try and relocate you. We have several thousand families living in the hills near here. I'm sure any one of them would be more than happy to take you in."

"That's it? The major thought you might use me as an interpreter or something. I'd like to help in any way I can."

The colonel smiled indulgently. "Maybe in a couple of years, son. Right now let's give the old-timers a chance, okay?"

Cody chewed on his bottom lip thoughtfully. Finally he stood and extended his hand. "It's been a pleasure, Colonel. If you'll have someone show me to my tent . . ."

"Certainly." The older man shook his hand again, then stepped outside and gave the waiting sergeant the order.

Cody followed the young man to a long tent with neat rows of cots set up inside. He waited until the soldier left and then darted across the camp to the medical tent.

"Can I help you?" A nurse holding a clipboard stopped him at the door.

"Uh, yeah. I'm looking for Major McLaughlin. She told me she'd be in here."

The nurse pointed to a door. "She'll be in there resting. The doctor just set her arm."

"Thanks." Cody turned and hurried through the door. Toni was lying on a cot, wearing a crisp new uniform with one sleeve missing. The smell of fresh, warm plaster of paris filled the air. Her arm was in a thick white cast up to her shoulder.

She smiled when she saw him. "How'd it go?"

"Your colonel is a jerk."

Toni looked confused. "What are you talking about?" She sat up on her good elbow. "Did he do something to you?"

"He wants to relocate me to live with a bunch of civilians."

"Is that all?" Toni lay back down. "That can't be so bad, can it?"

Cody set his jaw. "Listen, Toni. Luther Swift was a great man. He died so that I could be free. And there's a little girl back in that prison camp . . ."

"There's nothing you can do, Cody. Let the army take care of it. As soon as they knock out some of the enemy's strongholds they'll do what they can to help the prisoners."

Cody looked out the window, said nothing.

"You're going back, aren't you?"

He remained silent.

Toni sighed. "All right. They just rebroke my arm and I'll be useless for weeks. I know you won't wait until I can help." She took a pen and piece of paper she'd been using to write a letter and scribbled some numbers. "Here are two radio frequencies. If you go back and *if* they don't kill you and *if* you get into a position where you need help and *if* you can get to a radio, I'll be monitoring these freqs on a small receiver-transmitter at headquarters. I'll try to help any way I can."

Cody took the paper, looked at the numbers, then folded it and put it in his pocket. "Thank you . . ." He was gone and halfway to the perimeter of the compound, so he did not hear Toni say softly:

"No—I should be thanking you."

Book Two

★

RETURN

CHAPTER 1

The fire was hardly large enough to serve any real purpose. It had been such a long time since he'd made one that tonight he had decided to take the chance. But he was careful to stay back, well away from its light.

Cody Pierce was camped on the outskirts of the bombed-out city of Phoenix, looking for information or anything that might help him get the rest of the kids out of the prison.

It was past midnight. Cody scooped dirt onto the fire and was about to settle down to sleep when he heard a noise. Lying as still as possible, he strained to listen. Slow, heavy footsteps on gravel were coming up behind him.

Cody had chosen this place carefully. He silently crawled down into the rain-washed gully in front of him.

A flashlight scanned the area. "Harry, you idiot. He's gone."

Cody's ears perked up. These were fellow Americans. Maybe they could help him. He was about to call out to them when the second man spoke.

"It's not my fault. He must have heard us coming and run off."

"You better hope we find him, or at least another corpse to take this one's place. The CCR doesn't pay unless we deliver the bodies."

Cody swallowed. These men were mercenaries working for the enemy. Wasting no time, he inched down the narrow ditch and climbed out the other side. There was no cover here except the darkness. If he was lucky, he could slip away into the night un-noticed.

"That's far enough."

Cody froze. There was something familiar about that voice. A bright floodlight snapped on and shone in his eyes, making it impossible to see. He put his hands up.

"Well, what do you know? It's just a kid, boss. What should we do with him?"

The familiar voice spoke softly. "Put him in the truck. I've got special plans for this one."

CHAPTER 2

The door slammed on the panel truck and it started to move. Cody groped around on the floor. He soon found he wasn't alone. His fingers touched an arm. Hesitantly he reached for the face. It was cold and no breath came from the body's nostrils. When he pulled his hand back it was wet and sticky with blood.

Cody wiped his palms on his pants and slid back to his side of the truck. What kind of people were these, who killed their own countrymen for profit? He felt his way to the back

door to see what sort of lock held him prisoner. There wasn't one. There was no handle
on the inside at all.

He sat on his heels, thinking. If only he
had a weapon . . . Crawling back to the dead
man, he searched the body. An empty holster
was fastened to his belt. Next to the holster
was a small knife scabbard. Cody unsnapped
it and drew out a single-bladed hunting knife.

Quickly he removed the scabbard,
resheathed the knife and slid it into the top of
his right boot. He continued searching the
man and came up with a wallet. It was too
dark to read any of the contents but he could
feel some currency in the back of the billfold.
Knowing his captors would be suspicious if
the wallet was missing, he took the money
out, stuffed it in his other boot and put the
wallet back in the man's pocket.

The truck turned onto a paved road and
began speeding in the direction of the
bombed-out city. Cody crouched near the
back, hoping to take them by surprise when
they opened the door.

When the truck finally stopped, no one

opened the door. He could hear someone shouting and the squeaking of a gate being opened. Then they moved forward again but only for a short distance.

He heard what sounded like a dozen or more people running toward the back of the truck. There were too many to fight. Quickly he hid his knife again and was sitting complacently when the door was yanked open.

Rough hands grabbed his clothes and pulled him out of the truck. Cody tried to get a look at his surroundings. They were in some sort of compound surrounded by a tall chain-link fence. The men shoved him toward a large building that could once have been a warehouse.

He was taken through a side door and down a long hall. At the end of the hall they stopped. One of the men unlocked a brown metal door and held it open. The others shoved him in.

They pushed him so hard he fell to his knees, and by the time he was up and turned around, the door had been slammed shut and locked.

He took a deep breath and glanced around his cell. Only a little light filtered through the iron bars at the top of the cell door but it was enough for him to see that the room was empty except for a narrow cot at one end and a waste bucket near a drain in the middle of the room.

Taking the bucket, he flipped it upside down and stood on it so that he could see out of the small opening at the top of the door. They hadn't posted a guard and there was no one in the hall.

Cody felt in his shirt pocket for the short piece of wire he always carried. He inserted it in the keyhole and wiggled it slightly until he heard a barely audible click.

The door was heavy but opened easily. Cody pushed it slowly, trying not to make any noise. When he was out he closed it and started down the hall.

There were regular doors on both sides of the long hall and a set of double doors near the end. The outside door he had first come through had a glass pane in it. Cody inched up to it and looked out. Even at this early-morning hour there were men walking around out in the compound. It was obvious he couldn't go out the way he'd come in.

He sighed, frustrated. There had to be a way out. He'd just have to try all the doors until he found one that would work for him.

The set of double doors he'd seen earlier was the most intriguing. It had three different types of locks. He knew he shouldn't waste time but the door fascinated him. What was in there that was so important?

The padlock was easy for him and so was the key lock. The combination took a little more time. Cody turned the dial to the right and listened with his eyes closed. The first tumbler released. The second was just as simple. He took a deep breath and turned the knob back to the right, feeling for the last tumbler.

It fell.

Cody opened his eyes and gently pulled on the door. As he stepped inside, a voice spoke to him from the shadows.

"What took you so long, kid?"

Cody jumped sideways into a crouching

position, reached for his knife and waited for the man behind the voice to come out into the light. A figure stepped forward and Cody squinted up in shock at the familiar face. "I . . . I don't believe it. Franklin? Is that you?"

The tall dark man put his hand on Cody's shoulder. "In the flesh." Franklin's brown eyes twinkled as he looked back at the door. "I see you haven't lost your touch. Musta had one fine teacher."

CHAPTER 3

"I thought the CCR shot you. I mean, I know they did. I saw it with my own eyes."

"They shot me, all right." Franklin rubbed his side. "But no one cared enough to check and see if they'd done the job right. It took a while but I finally recovered and here I am."

The smile faded from Cody's face. He looked around the warehouse. It was a small weapons arsenal. Every kind of rifle, machine gun, bomb, grenade and missile launcher imaginable was stored there.

"What exactly are you doing, Franklin?" Cody asked suspiciously. "What are you doing working with these guys? They're killers, hired mercenaries . . ."

Franklin's eyes narrowed. "Don't be so quick to judge, Cody. Sometimes things aren't exactly what they seem."

A dog barked and a muscular young man fumbled with the already open locks before bursting in the door.

"Boss, the kid is gone just like you said he would be. I don't know how, but—" The dog, a stocky red and gray Australian heeler, snarled, and the young man noticed Cody standing slightly behind the door still holding the knife. He immediately aimed his submachine gun at the boy's head. "You want me to take him out?"

Franklin folded his arms. "Cody Pierce, meet Rico Hernandez."

Rico ran his left hand through his thick black hair, confused but still pointing the gun.

"Rico, Cody will be staying with us awhile. I want you to show him around the place. When you're done, bring him to my office. Cody and

I are old friends and we have a lot of catching up to do."

"Yes, sir. Uh, sir?" Rico scratched his dimpled chin. "You want me to show him everything?"

Franklin nodded and walked toward the doors. "Cody is to be treated like one of us. I'd trust him with my life."

CHAPTER 4

"Heel, Mike." The dog fell in behind the young soldier. "So you know the boss, huh?" Rico slung the gun over his shoulder. It rested there naturally as if it were part of him.

Cody nodded. "I used to. It's been a while, though."

"He's the best. He organized us. Probably saved most of us from being shot. Everybody here is about as loyal to him as you can get."

Cody followed Rico and the heeler through the warehouse. None of this made any sense.

He glanced at Rico's back. The man was young, probably not over twenty, easygoing and friendly. How could he and Franklin be involved in something like this?

Rico told the dog to sit and proudly pointed out some of the more specialized weapons. "We took these babies off a transport a couple of days ago." He threw back a tarp and pulled what looked like a rifle out of a crate. The barrel was huge and the sights weren't like any Cody had ever seen.

Rico tossed it to him. "Grenade launcher. Feel how light it is? Only weighs five pounds and has a range of over four hundred yards."

Cody's thoughts immediately went to the kids back at the prison camp. He chewed his lip and looked sideways at Rico. "Could you show me how to use this thing?"

"Sure. If the boss okays it." Rico smiled at him. "You got some private score to settle?"

Cody handed the gun back to him. "You could say that."

The rest of the tour included what was stored in the warehouse and the compound. The men who were awake in the barracks looked at him curiously but didn't ask any questions.

Outside, Cody glanced at the tall chain-link fence surrounding them. He noted the trucks and sand buggies parked near the gate. If he could get to one maybe he could hot-wire it and . . . no, he needed some of those weapons stored in the warehouse, and more than that, he needed someone to teach him how to use them. He'd just have to stay here awhile and bide his time.

"There's one other thing I still need to show you." Rico's voice broke into Cody's thoughts. "It's over here."

Rico led him to a small blockhouse with no windows or doors. "Stay, Mike." The dog stopped and sat. Rico unlocked the door and a blast of cold air hit them.

Cody walked inside. It was a freezer. Only instead of meat hanging from the ceiling, there were two bodies dressed in American military uniforms dangling from large metal hooks. A wave of nausea swept over Cody and he quickly stepped outside.

Rico followed. "You okay, kid?"

Cody whirled and glared at him. "How can you live with yourself? What kind of animals are you?"

The dog instantly jumped up, growling at Cody. Rico put his hand out. "It's okay, Mike. Chill out." He looked back at Cody. "The CCR pays good money for this scum. You wouldn't want us to go hungry, now, would you? Of course, I can't take any credit for it. It was all the boss's idea. Pretty clever, if you ask me."

Cody's eyes narrowed into tight slits. "I'd starve before I'd turn on one of our guys."

"Our guys?" Rico laughed. "Is that what you think? They weren't ours, they were CCR."

Cody looked confused. "I don't understand. They're wearing—"

"Of course they are, stupid. That's the beauty of it. We shoot one of theirs, dress him up, change his papers and collect the bounty. Not only does it pay well, it keeps the boss on their good side. As long as they think we're useful, they leave us alone."

"And all the weapons?" Cody raised an eyebrow.

"That's what we're really all about. We sort of . . . borrow them from the CCR and then redistribute them to the right parties."

CHAPTER 5

"Here he is, boss. I gave him the grand tour just like you told me." Rico showed Cody into an office that doubled as Franklin Stubbs' sleeping quarters.

Franklin was sitting at his desk, working on some papers. He put down his pencil and folded his arms. "Thanks, Rico. You can go get some rest now." When the door was closed, the dark-skinned man appraised the boy. "Well, what do you think of our little operation?"

Cody slid into one of the hard-backed chairs near the window. "I guess I understand things a little better now. Sorry about jumping to the wrong conclusions."

"No problem. It seems you and I have quite a few new and interesting things to discuss." Franklin pulled a poster out from under the paperwork on his desk. "Recognize this?"

Cody looked at the face. It was a kid with long blond hair and a red bandanna tied around his forehead. Underneath the picture in the Republic language it said: *Wanted for war crimes, dead or alive. The White Fox.*

Cody chewed his lip. "He sort of looks familiar."

Franklin laughed. "That's what I said when I first saw it. What did you do to the CCR to make them want you so bad?"

Cody shrugged. "Nothing much. Just took one of their prisoners and escaped from their stupid prison camp."

"Escaping was bad enough but the prisoner you took with you . . ." Franklin shook his head. "She wouldn't have been a rebel pilot, a Major Toni McLaughlin, by any chance, would she?"

"Could be."

Franklin laughed again. "You've changed, Cody. The kid I knew back in California was afraid of his own shadow. Now you're wanted for war crimes."

"The only crime I committed was making the CCR look like fools."

"That's enough, believe me. We get flyers on lots of people." Franklin leaned back in his chair and studied the boy. "What are you going to do now, Cody? If you're looking for a place to hide, you're more than welcome to stay here with us."

"Thanks. I might just take you up on that. But only for a while. I've got some business to take care of back at the camp."

"What kind of business?" Franklin scoffed. "You can't take on a whole prison camp by yourself. Stay with us. We can always use someone who's an old hand at making the CCR look bad."

Cody looked at the floor and thought, then raised his eyes. "I'll make you a deal. You have your guys teach me everything there is to know about the weapons stored in your warehouse and I'll do whatever you need me to do around here until it's time for me to leave."

Franklin stood up and extended his hand. "It's a deal, Cody—or should I call you White Fox?"

CHAPTER 6

"Try this move. Spin, and when you come around bring that right foot up beside my head. Do it like you mean it."

Cody took a deep breath. Without warning he spun around and brought his leg up hard. It caught Rico off balance and knocked him to the ground.

A wave of laughter rippled from the men behind them. Rico sat in the dirt and rubbed his cheek. "I think that's enough karate for today."

"What's the matter, Rico?" one of the men yelled. "Is your student showing you up?"

"Don't feel bad, son." Franklin walked over from the shade of the building where he was watching and helped Rico to his feet. "Cody has a way of leaving all his teachers in the dust."

Rico brushed the dirt off his pants. "In more ways than one, boss. Come on kid, let's go out to the firing range and work on your aim. We just brought in a small shipment of assault rifles."

"Sure thing, Rico. I'll go get Mike."

Franklin watched Cody walk across the grounds to the kennel. "Looks like the kid's doing pretty good."

"Good? That kid is a natural. Everything I show him he soaks up like a sponge. I never have to tell him anything twice. He's got a memory like a steel trap. He already knows how to fire, clean and disassemble every weapon we have on the place. Thompson's been teaching him hand-to-hand with a fighting knife, and as you can see, his progress in martial arts is flat amazing."

"Yeah, I see." Franklin pointed at the bright pink welt on Rico's face.

The radio operator came running from the office. "They're coming, boss. The scouts on the old I-10 highway just spotted them and called in. It's two official vehicles."

"Thanks, Walmer. Go ahead and sound the alarm." Franklin turned to Rico. "Keep Cody out of sight until the CCR is gone."

A loud siren went off and the men scrambled to get rid of contraband weapons and to busy themselves with innocent-looking tasks.

Rico ran across the grounds. "Come on, Cody. The big bad wolf is on his way and we don't want him to gobble you up."

Cody gave Mike a pat. "Stay here, boy. I'll be back for you later."

"That dog is getting to where he minds you better than he does me. I don't get it. I trained him from a pup."

"Dogs are incredibly smart, Rico. He just knows a good thing when he sees it."

Rico rolled his eyes. "Dognapper." The young soldier punched Cody playfully in the arm. "Come on. I better get you stowed away or the boss will have my hide."

He led Cody inside the warehouse and down some rickety steps into the unused dirt basement. "Be careful down here. There's a hole back there in the corner that goes to China. It must be at least fifty feet deep."

"Ooooohhhh." Cody made his voice sound spooky. "Is that where you throw the bodies you can't use to fool the CCR?"

"No, but that's where you're going to wind up if you don't stay down here and out of trouble until I come for you. Got it?"

Cody saluted. "Aye, aye, Captain."

"I'm not playing here, Cody. The boss doesn't like it when we do stupid things that might endanger the outfit."

"Quit worrying. I'm not going to do anything dumb."

"See to it that you don't." Rico pulled the door shut behind him and left Cody standing in the darkness.

Cody waited for almost a full minute before he followed. He took the steps two at a time and bounded down the hall to Franklin's office. Finding it empty, he closed the door and slowly pulled the window open a couple of inches so that he could hear what went on outside.

Two vehicles, an army truck and a long glossy black car, pulled through the gate and stopped in a cloud of dust. Several armed men got out of the truck and checked the area.

Then the driver of the first car jumped out and opened the back door. A man wearing a sharp black uniform with red trim on the collar stepped out.

Cody's breath caught in his throat for a moment. The man resembled a walking skeleton. His round, deep-set eyes were almost transparent and the skin on his slick bald head was pulled tight over his bony skull. An old scar puckered one cheek and a black mustache drooped from his upper lip.

Franklin approached the man and bowed the way all inferiors of the CCR were taught to do. "Welcome to our humble abode, Comrade Gollgath. What is it we can do for you today?"

The man analyzed him with a lean and

dangerous look, like a wolf among sheep. Then Cody saw the eyes travel to his window. Cody was well hidden behind a curtain but it still made his skin crawl.

Gollgath held a pair of thin leather gloves in his right hand, and he slapped them against his leg. "I understand that you have acquired four new specimens for inspection?"

"Yes, sir, we certainly have. Three are regular army but the fourth might interest you."

"How so?"

"He matches perfectly the description of that double agent on one of the flyers you sent out last month."

Gollgath seemed bored. "I'll be the judge of that, Stubbs. Show them to me."

Franklin and two of his men took the strange-looking officer and his driver to the blockhouse. The armed guards waited at the truck with their submachine guns in hand.

Cody watched Franklin show the skeleton man to the freezer. In a few moments they came out and the officer directed his driver to hand Franklin a small stack of money.

As they approached the car, Gollgath turned his grotesque face to Franklin. "Next time tell your men not to blow half the head off. If I can't recognize them, you don't get paid."

Franklin bowed. "Yes, Excellency. We'll work on that."

The driver opened the door and Gollgath started to step in. He paused. "Oh, and Stubbs . . . we are watching you. Don't get too greedy."

CHAPTER 7

"So, what did you think of Comrade Gollgath, or the Skull, as he's more commonly known?"

Cody frowned. "How did you know I was watching?"

Franklin pointed to his office window. "Pretty careless. You left it open."

"Sorry, Franklin. I was just—"

"I suggest you be a lot more careful when you go out with the men tonight."

"Me?" Cody's face lit up. "You're taking me with you on a raid?"

"You've got to learn sometime. I've been watching you these last few weeks and I think you're ready. The CCR is moving a load of missiles across the country tonight. They discovered them in an underground storage facility over in Nevada and we're going to intercept them."

"Good. When do we leave?"

"Hold on. Right now I want you to get some rest. Rico will find you when it's time."

Sleep was impossible. In fact, rest of any kind totally eluded him as his mind chewed on what lay ahead. When Rico came for him he was just as wide awake as he had been when he climbed up on his bunk.

A wad of black clothing hit him in the face. Rico laughed. "Heads up, Cody. The boss wants you to wear dark colors like the rest of us. It helps keep you from being spotted so easily."

Cody untied the bundle. The black suit resembled a pair of pajamas with a cord that tied around the waist. He looked at Rico, puzzled.

"It's another of the boss's strategies. The CCR thinks a group of partisans are hitting their weapons shipments. They've started calling us the Black Death after the suicide fighters that fought the CCR back in the early days." Rico shrugged. "So far it's kept them off our trail."

"Whatever works." Cody wriggled into the black clothes and waited for Rico's next instructions.

"Go on over to the warehouse and wait for me. We'll need to outfit you with a weapon and paint that shiny white face of yours. I'll be along just as soon as I take care of something for the boss."

Cody felt lighter in his new clothes. He trotted across the compound to Franklin's office. The big man wasn't there so he decided to try the radio room.

A few feet from the closed door he stopped in his tracks. Walmer, the radio operator, was on the air speaking to someone in the Republic language.

Cody edged closer to the door.

"No, Comrade. I don't have access to that. . . . I'm telling you it's something big. No, I can't talk now. . . . When I know for sure . . . Yes . . . I better go now before anyone . . ."

Cody slid down the hall a few yards and then walked casually toward the radio room. He knocked on the door and heard Walmer drop something.

"Just a minute. . . . Come in."

"Hi, Walmer." Cody's eyes measured the short, round-bodied man. His skin was pasty and his cotton-white hair stuck out under his cap. He fidgeted nervously with some papers while Cody walked around him. "I was looking for Franklin. You seen him?"

"Ah . . . no. He hasn't been here all morning. If I see him, though, I'll tell him you're looking for him."

"Thanks." Cody started to leave but turned at the door. "That was some strange jabbering you were doing just now on the radio, Walmer. What was it?"

"That? Oh, it was just routine. I was reporting in to the CCR. They require us to do that every so often so they can keep tabs on us."

"Really?" Cody faked a smile. "Well, you're pretty good at it. In fact, you sound just like one of them."

CHAPTER 8

"How long has Walmer been with the organization?"

Cody had asked to speak to Franklin in private a few minutes before the team was scheduled to leave. Standing across from the big man in a corner of the warehouse, the boy was hardly recognizable. His face was covered with camouflage paint, a snub-nose submachine gun loaded with thirty-two rounds of ammunition hung from his shoulder and a

Special Forces combat knife was strapped on his belt.

"He came in a few days before we found you. Of course, we've been careful not to let him in on everything. He doesn't know any of our sources or about changing the uniforms of the CCR. I assume you have a good reason for asking?"

"Did you know he speaks fluent Republic?"

"That's what got him one of the radio operator jobs. We needed somebody who could talk to them. What's your point, Cody?"

"I heard him talking to the CCR today. It didn't sound right. I think you should watch him."

Franklin raised his hand and summoned Rico.

"You need something, boss?"

Franklin spoke softly near his ear. "Walmer is a plant. Tell Gunner to get rid of him."

"Wait." Cody grabbed Franklin's sleeve. "Aren't you going to make sure?"

Franklin's eyes turned hard. "This is reality, Cody. We're in a war here and I don't have the luxury of waiting. By the time we find out, it could be too late for all of us. Understand?"

Cody looked at the floor. A few minutes before, he had been positive that Walmer was a spy working for the other side. So positive that he had turned him in. But now, what if he was wrong . . . the thought trailed off.

Franklin wished them luck and ordered the team to the trucks. Cody moved mechanically. He fell in behind the men and somehow made his way outside.

Thompson gave him a hand up into the back of the truck. "Stick with me, kid. I'll make sure you don't get your rump shot off."

Rico was the last one in. He sat down across from Thompson. "Don't worry about Cody. The boss wouldn't have chosen him to go on this run if he couldn't hold up his end of it."

CHAPTER 9

As the trucks sped through the night, Cody thought about Walmer. What if he wasn't a plant? What if . . .

Rico touched his arm and whispered. "You did the right thing, kid. There are a lot of lives at stake here. Now it's done with. Put it out of your mind. Think about the mission. These guys will all be watching you. Don't let us down, okay?"

Cody forced himself to concentrate on the briefing Franklin had given them. They were on their way to the train depot at Wilcox. Rico and another man named Martin had the job of slipping in and checking out the site. When they gave the all clear, the rest of them were supposed to come in, take out the guards and load the missiles.

Franklin had especially wanted Cody to go along because of the wall safe in the depot office. It would be his job to crack it, gather the contents and meet the rest of them back at the truck.

Three hours passed before the trucks finally pulled off on a side road and turned out their lights. One by one the men silently jumped out.

Rico and Martin slipped down the hill toward the depot lights. The rest of them crawled to the edge of the road and watched, waiting for the signal.

Cody's palms started sweating. He'd never actually killed an enemy before. There was the farmer he'd stabbed with the pitchfork. But that hadn't been planned and he wasn't positive the farmer had died.

He felt a firm tap on his shoulder and

glanced down the hill. A light flashed three times. Rico and Martin were in.

Thompson led the way down the slope. There were eight of them altogether, including Rico and Martin. Franklin never sent very large teams. The idea was to take the enemy by surprise, get the job done and get out without being caught.

Martin was waiting for them at the bottom of the hill. "The troops sent to guard the missiles are housed over there in that building for the night," he whispered, pointing to a square shack on the other side of the tracks. "There are six guards in front of the freight car where the missiles are stored." He turned to Cody. "The depot looks empty. Give us a couple of minutes to take out the guards, then go in."

"Let's get to it." Thompson and two men went one way and Martin and the rest went another. Cody was left standing alone, not quite sure what to do.

He waited, counting off the seconds, took a deep breath and haltingly made his way to the depot. When he reached the outside wall, he flattened himself against it and listened. After a long moment he peeked around the corner. The team had already dispatched the guards and was unloading the missiles.

Cody smiled to himself. Maybe this mission wasn't going to be so bad after all.

As quietly as he could he crept across the wooden porch and tried the depot door. It was locked. Cody reached in his pocket for his lockpick and in moments the door swung open.

A dim yellow light hung from the lobby ceiling. Cody searched the room. Franklin had told him the wall safe would be in an office through a door to his right. He found the door, softly opened it and looked for the safe. It was there just as Franklin had said.

Slipping his gun sling over his head, he laid the submachine gun on the floor beside the safe. There was barely enough light from the other room for him to see what he was doing. Franklin had given Cody a small flashlight but cautioned him to use it only in an emergency. They had received the same instructions about their guns. If at all possible, they were to pull off the entire job without a shot to avoid waking the rest of the guards.

The safe looked like one of many he and Franklin had opened back in Los Angeles a couple of years before. Cody dropped to his knees and went to work. The first tumbler fell without a hitch. But the second one was stubborn. Cody missed it and had to start over.

He held his breath and turned the knob again. It fell on the right, then on the left and then, very slowly, listening with all his might, Cody turned the knob back to the right and finally heard the last tumbler drop.

Cody let out his breath and pulled the safe door open. There was no time to check the contents. He grabbed at everything and began stuffing it into a canvas pouch Franklin had given him for the purpose.

"Hurry it up, kid."

Cody jumped and grabbed for his gun. He'd been concentrating so hard he hadn't heard Thompson come in behind him.

"You shouldn't do that," Cody whispered angrily.

"Do what?" Thompson whispered back from the doorway. "Scare the baby?"

Cody ignored him and went back to cleaning out the safe.

"I have you covered." A bright light snapped on in the other room. "Turn around slowly and put your hands on your head," a voice commanded.

Cody realized whoever was in the next room couldn't see him kneeling on the floor because Thompson's large frame was blocking the doorway. He quietly crawled to the side while Thompson put his hands up and turned to face the voice.

"Step over here, away from the door."

The soldier kept his gun on Thompson while he edged toward the room to see what his new captive had been up to. He spotted the open safe and cursed in the Republic language, then turned. "You will be shot for this—of course, you would have been shot in any case."

The instant the CCR soldier turned his back, Cody was up. In one motion he slipped the combat knife from the sheath and threw himself forward, the knife in front of him like a short sword. It was all automatic and later he knew that if he'd thought about it he couldn't have done it. The knife seemed to disappear into the back of the soldier and the man gasped, a tight breath, half turned to see what had hit him and fell forward and down on his face. The soldier moved a moment and was still. Cody stood, staring at the knife sticking out of the middle of the dead man's back. He could not make himself move. Not an inch.

Thompson was not idle. He leaned over, made sure the soldier was dead and then smiled up at Cody. "You saved me. . . ." He was going to say something more but at that moment Rico sprinted into the depot, breathing hard, with an angry frown on his face. "What's the holdup in here?"

He saw the soldier lying facedown on the floor and glanced across at Cody, who was still poised to attack. "Is everybody okay?"

"Thanks to the kid here," Thompson said. "He's something else. How old did you say he is again?"

"He's fourteen." Rico grinned. "But he's a *mean* fourteen."

CHAPTER 10

"Come on, Mike. Here, boy." Cody whistled and called to the big dog, who had run off after a rabbit.

Mike bounded up behind him, nearly knocking him over. Cody knelt and playfully patted his head. "Where's the rabbit? I guess you failed in your mission, didn't you? That's okay. With all that money from the depot safe, Franklin said he'd be buying everybody steaks for a while. What do you think about that?"

The heeler licked Cody's face.

"Yeech. You don't have to be that appreciative." Cody stood up and adjusted his gun across his shoulder. Nowadays, he never left the compound without it. The gun, along with the combat knife he'd retrieved from the back of the dead soldier, had become a part of him and he felt strange when the weapons weren't with him.

It had been almost three weeks since the depot mission. Thompson had bragged on him until it became embarrassing. Franklin was proud too. Even though he didn't say much, Cody could see it in his eyes. Cody was not proud—that is, he was proud that he'd saved Thompson, but he had dreamt several times about it, dreamt about the knife going into the soldier's back, and he always awakened in a sweat.

Rico continued to teach him martial arts and how to use the various weapons stored in the warehouse. But Cody felt restless. His thoughts turned more and more to Sidoron's prison camp and his plans to try and rescue the kids there.

In the afternoons he had started taking long walks with Mike. He'd discovered a small window in the basement that was just big enough for the two of them to squeeze through. When he needed to think, they slipped out into the desert to be alone.

He'd decided that he had put things off long enough. Today he had to tell Franklin about his decision to leave the organization. It would be hard. The men at the warehouse had become like a family to him. He knew Franklin would try to talk him out of it, maybe even volunteer some of the guys to go along and help.

Cody straightened. He'd just have to be firm. What they were doing at the warehouse was extremely important to the resistance effort and he couldn't allow them to sacrifice it for his plans.

"Let's go, Mike. I guess I better get it over with. Who knows, if things work out for me, they might even let me come back someday."

He glanced down at the dog. His ears were pointed and the hair on his back bristled.

"What's the matter?"

Cody listened. He could hear faint, rapid popping.

Gunfire.

It was coming from the direction of the warehouse base. He started running.

CHAPTER 11

Cody lay flat on the ground twenty yards from the fence in the cover of some low bushes. A shiny black car and a transport truck were parked inside the chain-link. Republic soldiers with machine guns were moving around freely in the compound.

Bodies were lying everywhere. The men inside had been taken totally by surprise and the CCR soldiers had cut them down where they stood.

Cody felt sick. He scanned the area. Something was hanging from the flagpole in the center of the compound. He squinted to see it better. It was a man. A tall man with dark skin.

Franklin.

Cody closed his eyes and buried his face in the sand. It wasn't fair. He should have been there when it happened. Maybe he would have been able to help or would have seen something suspicious and warned them.

A low growl came from behind him where he'd told Mike to stay. Cody looked up. Goll gath, the Skull, stepped into the black car and it whipped around and sped out the gate.

The soldiers who had come in the truck had remained behind to guard the place.

"What do we do now?" Cody whispered. He sat on his heels, trying to think. What would Franklin want him to do? The warehouse had several large shipments of guns, ammunition and missiles inside waiting to be moved to the partisans and rebels. Surely the CCR had discovered them by now and had a call in to headquarters to have them removed.

Cody put his arms around the dog. "We're all that's left to stop them. . . ." He leaned back and watched the black car disappear down the highway. "And I say if we can't have the stuff in that warehouse then nobody's going to get it. You stay here, Mike. I've got a little fire to start."

CHAPTER 12

The small basement window was half-open, the way he'd left it. Cody inched up to it and peered inside. It was too dark to see. He listened but didn't hear anyone moving around.

Feet first, he wiggled down through the window and dropped lightly to the dirt floor. Then he worked his way around the deep pit in the corner and over to the rickety wooden steps. Climbing them quickly, he stopped on the landing and pushed the door open a tiny crack.

Two CCR soldiers were standing guard down the hall in front of the warehouse's double doors. He pulled the door shut and rubbed his forehead. Somehow he had to get rid of those guards. Shooting them was out of the question. A dozen more would rush in if he tried it. If he was very lucky he might take one of them with karate but probably not both.

An idea formed in his mind. Hurrying back down the steps, he felt in the dirt for rocks and put several in his pocket. Then he raced up to the landing and opened the door again.

The two guards obviously didn't consider themselves in any danger. They were smoking and talking about the fight to take the compound.

Cody let out a low whistle.

Both guards turned and looked in his direction. He deliberately left the basement door open a crack and darted down the steps to hide.

He heard them coming. The door opened and one of them yelled down, "Who's there?"

Silence.

Cody stood completely still, not even breathing, hiding under the stairs—waiting.

"There's nothing here, Comrade." One of the guards started to leave. "It was just the wind."

Cody took out a couple of the pebbles and tossed them at the corner of the room.

The guards immediately rushed to the bottom of the steps. One of them took a flashlight from a clip on his belt and pointed it around the room. He spotted the half-open window.

"I must report this." He handed the light to the other guard. "Stay here. If anyone comes through that window, shoot them."

Cody tossed a few more rocks near the corner. Both guards quickly moved toward the noise, their guns pointed, ready.

When they were standing by the edge of the pit, Cody made his move. He sprang out from his hiding place, putting all the energy he could muster into his legs, and charged like a mad bull.

He hit them hard. The guards lost their balance. One fell screaming to the bottom.

The other dropped his rifle and was falling in when he managed to grab Cody's leg.

Cody fell backward. He frantically clawed the dirt around him for something to hang on to. He was losing ground, sliding toward the edge. Somehow he had to break the guard's grip. Using his other foot, he drew back and savagely kicked the guard in the face. The soldier lost his grip, started to swear and then dropped into the hole.

When he hit, Cody heard a light thud. Then the basement was eerily quiet.

Cody sat up and looked over the edge. The soft glow from the guard's flashlight showed the outline of their tangled bodies far below and Cody felt a slight nausea. They looked so small. . . .

Then he thought of Franklin hanging on the flagpole and he shook his head and went back to work.

CHAPTER 13

Entering the warehouse was a snap. The CCR had blown the locks off, so all Cody had to do was slip inside and go to work.

He found a grenade launcher and a small case of grenades. Then he grabbed a machine gun and belt.

"This ought to about do it." Cody carried his stack of weapons to the hall and hurried across to Franklin's office.

From the window he counted the soldiers who had been left to guard the warehouse.

There were fourteen in the open and he guessed a few more would be in the barracks.

His position was good. From where he stood he could see the entire compound. Quickly he opened the crate holding the grenades and loaded the launcher. Sliding the window open, he took aim at the largest group of CCR and without thinking pulled the trigger.

The wall of the building where they stood exploded. Bodies flew into the air and landed motionless ten feet away.

Not waiting for the enemy to recover, he launched one grenade after another until he couldn't see anything but dust and flying debris. Then he set the bipod of the machine gun on the windowsill and fired randomly across the ground.

He heard someone yell as if they'd been hit. There was a movement near the barracks. Cody squeezed off several rounds in that general direction and saw a soldier spin around and fall to the ground.

He fired until nothing was moving. Taking the last of his grenades and his two guns, he moved down the hall to the door leading out into the compound.

He swallowed, opened the door and dashed around the corner of the warehouse, pointing his submachine gun in front of him and looking for anything that moved. To keep the confusion going he shot another grenade in the direction of the blockhouse.

The cement wall of the blockhouse took the force of the explosion and bits of concrete flew into the air. Cody climbed on top of a truck and jumped onto the roof of the offices. He set up the machine gun and waited.

To his right he heard a noise like someone trying to climb the drainpipe. He crawled across the roof on his stomach, aimed the short barrel of his submachine gun over the edge and straight down along the pipe and fired. There was a startled yell and a thump when the soldier hit the ground.

Quickly Cody went back to his position at the edge of the roof and scanned the compound. There was a moment of eerie silence, broken only by the sound of flames licking at a wooden bulletin board in front of the barracks.

Is that all of them? he thought. Are there no more soldiers? He was startled by a sharp crack as wood at the edge of the roof splintered and chipped off from the force of a bullet. He saw quick movement at one of the barracks windows and fired a grenade that exploded harmlessly against the side of the building. He loaded the launcher and held it a bit higher and was gratified to see the grenade go through a window. There was a muffled explosion inside and he waited.

No more shots came.

Cody waited still longer, watching the windows, but nothing more moved and he slipped off the roof onto the truck and then to the ground.

He checked the magazine in his gun and walked around the compound. Nobody moved. Mike had chewed the tie cord and was digging a hole near the gate, trying to get in. Cody opened it for him and the dog rushed inside, sniffing at the bodies strewn across the ground.

Cody followed him to the flagpole and lowered Franklin's bullet-riddled body. He cried openly and kept working though his stomach was tight and he felt like throwing up.

Gently he laid his friend on the ground and looked around for Rico. Partly because of the destruction he'd caused and partly because the CCR had done such a thorough job, it was impossible for him to identify anyone else.

Knowing his time was short, Cody went back into the warehouse and started carrying weapons and supplies to one of the sand buggies. The radio and extra cans of gasoline were the last items he loaded before he went back into the storage area for the final time.

Rico had explained the mechanisms of the various bombs that came through the warehouse, though Cody had never been allowed to mess with them. He moved to the Big Red, an older bomb used to create landing pads for helicopters in thick forest. Rico had told him the bomb had an enormous concussion and would level everything for fifty yards in all directions. If he could set the bomb off here in the building it should easily detonate the rest of the stuff in the warehouse.

On one wall, on shelves, there were smaller charges of plastic explosive and he found a timer and detonator where Rico had pointed them out. He put the small charge on top of the bomb and set the timer for fifteen minutes.

He ran out the door and hopped into the sand buggy. "Come on, Mike. We better make tracks before that timer runs out."

The heeler jumped into the front seat and Cody started the motor and roared out the gate. He stayed on the pavement until he came to the first dirt road. It led to a fork and he decided to take the less traveled way.

The sand buggy was four miles away, moving fast on a back road, when the ground shook and there was a deafening explosion. Cody hit the brakes, pulled off and looked back.

A flat-topped mushroomlike cloud took over the sky. First it was white and then it changed to dark gray and he sat for a long time, the dog panting softly next to him, and thought of all that had ended there under that cloud.

CHAPTER 14

Mike barked. Cody opened his heavy eyelids and swerved around a boulder in the road, barely missing it. He wiped his eyes, realizing that he had fallen asleep at the wheel. "Whew! Time to stop, boy, before I kill us both."

It was late evening. He had driven the back roads all through the night and most of the next day without stopping for food or rest.

To his right was a piece of a gate with a sign that read DOUBLE B HORSE FARM. Cody pushed the gate open with his bumper and drove into a pretty meadow surrounded by broken-down white wooden fences. He stopped the buggy at the top of a grassy knoll and turned off the motor.

Reaching into his supplies, he pulled out a pair of binoculars. The CCR had leveled the ranch house but an old barn with part of its roof missing was still standing.

"Looks like that's our motel for the night, boy."

He drove up to the barn and hastily got out to open the large wooden doors, then drove inside and parked.

Mike leaped down and ran outside to explore. Cody looked around warily. The barn had a high ceiling with a loft above. A few bales of rotting hay were stacked in one corner next to some old tractor parts. It looked sturdy enough.

Cody yawned as the heeler trotted in. "I could sleep for a year but I guess I better feed us first." He reached into his pack for a couple of cans of stew. "Here, boy. Come and get it."

Mike wagged his tail. He sat down and waited patiently for Cody to open one of the cans.

From somewhere above them, a few wisps of hay trickled down between the slats of the loft. Mike's hair bristled and he let out a low growl. The dog started for the ladder but stopped when Cody called him back.

"It's okay, boy," Cody said in a loud voice. "There's no one here but you and me. Come back and eat your supper."

Reluctantly Mike moved away from the ladder and back to Cody's side.

"Stay," Cody commanded. He took his gun, edged to the ladder and slowly climbed it.

The instant his head cleared the top of the loft something heavy hit him full in the face and knocked him backward off the ladder.

CHAPTER 15

"Call your dog off."

Cody's hand went to the back of his aching head. He gasped for air and strained against the pain to pull himself to a sitting position. The wind had been knocked out of him and the back of his head stung as if it were on fire.

The voice came from above. He opened one eye and tried to concentrate.

"Call your dog off, kid, so I can see how bad you're hurt."

Cody focused on the voice. A girl about his age was standing on the ladder. She was dressed in tattered blue jeans and a grimy T-shirt. Her dark hair was pulled back in a tangled ponytail. Mike had her trapped and wasn't about to let her get down. Every time she moved he bared his teeth.

"Leave her alone, Mike."

The dog backed away a few feet but watched the girl suspiciously.

She climbed down and brushed the hay off her jeans. "Thanks. Sorry about hitting you with that sack of feed. These days you just can't be too careful, you know. When I first saw you in those army clothes with that gun I got worried. I didn't know you were just a kid. Want me to take a look at your head?"

Cody tried to speak but suddenly everything went black.

The next time he opened his eyes it was morning. The sun was shining brightly through the hole in the barn roof. He touched his head. It still ached but it had been bandaged and a piece of gauze was wrapped around his forehead to hold the bandage in place.

He heard a noise and turned toward it. The girl had most of his equipment out on the barn floor and was rummaging through it.

"Hey. What do you think you're doing?"

She whirled around. "So, you came back to the living. For a while there, I wasn't too sure which way it would go."

"Get out of my stuff."

The girl put her hands on her hips. "Well, that's gratitude for you. I fix your bleeding skull and you want me to stay out of your stuff."

Cody managed to sit up. "My head wouldn't be bleeding if it weren't for you."

"And I couldn't have found the bandages in your first-aid kit if I hadn't gone through your things."

"Where's Mike? We gotta get out of here."

"Mike? Oh, your dog. I fed him his breakfast and he went out for a nature walk."

"Put all that stuff back in the buggy. I have to leave right away."

"Why? The CCR hot on your trail?"

Cody frowned. "What makes you think that?"

"Just a wild guess. Most people don't carry

around a small arsenal with them when they travel. I figure you probably borrowed it from them."

Cody grabbed a ladder rail and pulled himself to his feet. The building threatened to spin away from him.

"You better take it easy for a while. You have a nasty cut on your head."

"Hummpphh." Cody glared at her and took a faltering step toward the sand buggy.

"Some people . . ." The girl moved to his side. "Let me help you." She took his arm and led him to the front of the buggy. "Now what?"

Cody shook her off. "Now I'm going to load my stuff and get outta here."

"Sure you are. Look, I never said I wouldn't put it back. I just wanted to see what was in it. You wait here and I'll load it for you. Then we can leave."

"We? You're not coming with me."

"Of course I am. You can hardly see, much less drive. And I can't stay here anymore. The CCR is crawling all over the area."

"Listen, whatever your name is . . ."

"It's Rachel. Rachel Vega. We used to live not too far from here. One day the CCR flew over and bombed our place. I was out riding at the time. I think I'm the only survivor in this whole valley."

"I'm sorry, Rachel. But I'm going to a very hard place—there's a chance I'm not coming back."

"I assume you're going to use this stuff against the CCR, right?"

Cody nodded.

"Then I'm coming with you. So far all I've done since they killed my family is scrounge for food and hide from them. If I go with you maybe I can change that. Maybe I can help— get back at them."

Cody thought about the way he had felt when Colonel Wyman told him he was too young to do anything and wanted to send him to a safe house in the mountains. Cody studied Rachel. It was against his better judgment but she had a determined look on her face.

"Well, hurry it up, then. We gotta get these supplies loaded or we'll never get out of here."

CHAPTER 16

Rachel sat on the driver's side. Mike was between them, still panting from his run. Cody looked across the dog's back. Rachel was studying the dash and gears.

"Have you ever driven before?"

She turned the key. "Sure . . . plenty." The sand buggy jerked forward and stopped. "Only before it's always been on my dad's tractor. But don't worry. I'll get the hang of it."

"Reverse is over here." Cody pointed to the floor.

"Right." Rachel shoved it into reverse and let out the clutch and they flew backward out of the barn.

"Not so fast. Take it easy."

The transmission made a grinding noise as she found the right gear and turned the buggy around. "There. I told you I'd get the hang of it. Which way are we going?"

"Take a right when we get to the gate. First chance we get we need to cut across open country. We're headed for the middle of nowhere, Rachel, to visit a nice little prison camp I used to call home." He put his head back and closed his eyes.

"I knew it. You're him, aren't you? The White Fox. I saw a poster on you in town. Did you really do all those things they say you did?"

Cody didn't open his eyes. "My name is Cody Pierce. And you shouldn't believe everything you read. Especially if it's written by the CCR."

"Why do they call you that? You don't look much like a fox." She glanced over at him. "Maybe it's your hair. If you washed it . . ."

The sand buggy hit a rock in the road and bounced off.

"Pay attention to your driving." Cody opened one eye. "In fact, why don't you turn off here? They won't be as likely to find us if we stay off the roads."

The sand buggy was built for rough terrain and bounced up an incline and over a sloping hill. Rachel jammed on the brakes. "Do you know how to use the guns and stuff in the backseat?"

"Yeah. Why?" Cody sat up. In front of them was a CCR patrol. And it was headed straight for them.

CHAPTER 17

"Do you think they've seen us?" Rachel asked nervously.

Bullets sprayed the ground in front of them.

"I think they've seen us. Get this thing turned around."

Rachel put it in gear and the buggy jumped forward.

"Reverse, Rachel. Put it in reverse."

"I'm trying." Suddenly the buggy lurched backward at full speed. They withdrew down the same incline they'd just come up. When they reached the road, Rachel slammed the buggy into a forward gear and tore off with the gas pedal to the floor.

"We'll never be able to outrun them," Cody shouted. "Pull off into that bunch of trees."

"Are you crazy?" Rachel yelled "They'll capture us for sure if we stop."

"Do it," Cody commanded. He was already turned around and reaching into one of the boxes he'd packed especially for such an oc- casion.

Rachel whipped behind the trees. "What's that thing?"

"It's one of the only high-tech weapons that ever came through the warehouse. It fires laser bolts." Cody lifted a strange, shiny metal gun from the back and stepped out of the buggy. His head started pounding and it was all he could do to keep from falling.

"I'll help. Tell me what to do." Rachel took the long-barreled gun. "Do I load it with something?"

Cody held out his hand. "These go in the top."

Rachel quickly grabbed two hard black objects that resembled pieces of coal and stuffed them into the gun. "Now what?"

Cody leaned on the buggy for support. He gently took the big gun and aimed it at the road. "Here." He handed her his submachine gun. "Take this. Get behind that tree, point it at anything that moves and just pull the trigger."

Almost before he got the words out, the patrol trucks stormed over the incline. Cody aimed his weapon and fired.

Something resembling a blue lightning bolt hit the patrol and took out the first two trucks, incinerating them. A few of the soldiers from the last truck jumped clear just as Cody fired again, leaving it a smoking pile of ashes.

To his right he could hear Rachel firing at the soldiers who were running for cover.

What was left of the patrol started shooting back. Cody aimed at a stand of trees. When the laser hit them, they boiled into flame.

"Get in the buggy, Rachel. It's time to leave."

Cody carefully laid the laser gun in the back and crawled in beside Mike. Rachel turned the key and tore down the hill.

"We did it, Cody," Rachel said, beaming. "Nobody ever beats the CCR but we did it. Cody? What's the matter?"

He didn't answer. Rachel glanced over at him. The front of his shirt was wet with blood.

CHAPTER 18

Cody was dreaming. A Blackhawk III chopper with a medevac team was landing near them. The pilot smiled warmly at him. It was Toni. She told him not to worry and then she put a cold compress on his burning forehead.

The medics were attempting to put him on a stretcher but his shoulder was so sore that the slightest movement sent pain jolting through his body.

Something wet and slimy licked his chin.

His eyes fluttered open and he saw Mike's big, furry, concerned face.

The dog barked and Rachel ran to his side. "How are you feeling?"

"I . . . think I've felt better. My mouth tastes like cotton. Could I have some water?"

"Water is one thing we have plenty of— we're camped beside a river. Be right back."

"I'm not going anywhere." Cody couldn't remember when he'd felt so awful, unless it was the time Sidoron had burned him with his cigar and then beaten him senseless.

Rachel brought a canteen and held it to his lips. "Here you go. Take it easy." She tipped it up and waited for him to swallow. "You talk in your sleep. Did you know that?"

Cody moved his head. "Thanks for the water."

"No problem. Who's Toni? Your girlfriend?"

"She's a friend. Where did you say we were?"

"I've hidden the buggy in some trees. It's out of fuel. If my geography serves me right, we're camped by the Gila River."

Cody tried to sit up but he was too weak.

"You shouldn't move. You took a bullet in the shoulder. I washed it and did the best I could with it, but frankly it looks pretty bad."

"Thanks for the encouraging words."

"I'm just trying to be honest. By the way, I'm sorry about your friends at the warehouse. It sounded awful."

"Is there anything I didn't talk about while I was out?"

"Nope, I think you about covered everything."

"How long have we been here?"

"A night and a day. I found this place just before dark yesterday."

"Get me up, Rachel. We can't stay here. After that bit with the laser gun, the CCR isn't just going to forget about us."

"You're staying right where you are. Do you know how long it took me to stop the bleeding in your shoulder? Besides, if you're bent on killing yourself anyway, why not do it here?"

Cody moaned in agony. "Help me, Rachel. I can't do it by myself."

Rachel put a restraining hand on his arm. "I know you're a big tough guy but . . ."

He had half risen but he was too weak and fell back, his eyes only half-open, and Rachel smiled as she watched him drift back to sleep.

Rachel felt Cody stir beside her. She and Mike were lying close to him to keep him warm. In the night he'd gotten chills and his fever seemed higher. She'd emptied the packs but couldn't find any blankets, so she'd piled the canvas bags on him and ordered Mike to lie down next to him.

Cody moaned deliriously and threatened a guy named Sidoron and then rambled wildly about someone hanging from a flagpole.

A twig snapped behind her.

Mike raised his head. Rachel felt for Cody's gun. She'd deliberately laid it beside her before going to sleep but it was too late. They were suddenly surrounded by a circle of men, dressed in animal skins and holding torches.

Rachel pulled the gun around and pointed it at the man in front. "What do you want here?"

The man moved forward. He was dressed only in a tanned hide tied loosely around his waist. Mike growled but didn't attack. He allowed the man to kneel by Cody and examine his wound.

"This boy is dying. We can help." The man signaled for two of his men. They lifted Cody gently and carried him to the edge of the circle.

"Wait. Why should we trust you?"

The man turned. "Do you want him to live?"

Rachel hesitated. "What about our things?" The man inclined his head and the others started gathering Cody's belongings. Rachel double-checked to make sure nothing was left; then she and Mike followed them along the river and up a steep hill.

The sun came out and the hill turned into a mountain. Now they were in the middle of a wilderness. The grass was green and the trees were tall. Above them were high red bluffs practically hidden by the wild overgrowth.

The group stopped at the foot of the cliffs and Rachel sat down to catch her breath. No one spoke to her. They went about their business as if she weren't there.

At last the largest man in the group put down his spear and stood still while the others placed Cody on his back, tying the boy's hands and feet securely together.

Two men moved some branches and exposed a homemade wooden ladder next to the cliff. The big man started up it.

Rachel put her hand over her eyes to block the sun's rays and looked up. There were several ladders going all the way to the top of the cliffs.

One of the men indicated that it was her turn to climb. She held on to Mike. "What about our dog? He can't go up there."

"The dog will stay. We have hidden your

supplies in the woods near our horses. He can guard them until your friend is better. Don't worry. Our hunting parties will bring him food from time to time." The man took the gun from around her neck. She started to protest but he interrupted. "Too heavy. I'll carry it."

Rachel nodded wearily and started climbing. Halfway up she looked at the ground and started feeling dizzy.

"Look up only," the man behind her ordered.

Rachel took his advice and soon found herself on a ledge. She stumbled onward and stepped through a curtain of brush.

She stopped and held her breath. It was amazing. Hidden deep in the heart of the cliff was a whole village. Children were running and playing while women dressed in skins sat near cave entrances making baskets and cooking.

The scene was right out of prehistoric times, except that these people spoke English and one of them now carried Cody's submachine gun.

"Rise and shine, Cody. Breakfast is ready."

"Uggh. Get that lumpy stuff away from me. For the past two weeks all I've had to eat is mush. Can't you get me some real food?"

Rachel frowned. "Keep your voice down. These people saved your life and now you're complaining about the food? And it's been three weeks. You were unconscious for most of the first one."

"Whatever. Tell the big cheese to give me my clothes back and I'll go get my own food."

Cody shyly pulled the hide blanket up a little higher on his chest.

"His name is Samuel. And if it wasn't for him . . ."

"Your young friend may be right." Samuel stepped through the small cave entrance. He was a tall man with skin tanned by the sun. His blue eyes seemed to laugh when he spoke. "If the patient is complaining, it's a sure sign that he's improving."

Cody fidgeted with the edge of the hide. "It's not that I don't appreciate everything you've done. Rachel told me how your hunting party found us and brought us here. It must have been a hard decision to expose your people to outsiders like that. You've got your own little world up here. A perfect hiding spot from the CCR."

Samuel shrugged. "It wasn't hard. You're Americans and so are we." He turned to go. "I'll bring your clothes. But take it slow, okay? We didn't heal you so that you could start moving around too soon and make yourself sick again."

"Thanks, Samuel."

"I guess you want me to take this back to the cook?" Rachel held out the bowl.

Cody made a face and sighed. "Oh, I guess I can force it down one more time. Heck, I used to eat worse than this all the time in the prison camp."

Rachel handed him the bowl. "Are you still planning on going back there?"

"Why wouldn't I? Nothing's changed."

"It's just that . . . never mind. When were you thinking of leaving?"

"As soon as my arm can do what I tell it to." Cody stopped eating. "Look, Rachel, you don't have to come. I can tell you like it here. This is my own private war. Stay with these people. They'll be glad to have you."

"Don't talk like that. You need me. At least you have so far. You'd probably be lying in a ditch somewhere if you hadn't met me."

Cody rubbed the back of his head. "Or had one less concussion."

A young boy stepped into the cave carrying Cody's clothes. "Uncle Samuel said to bring these." He stared at Cody's wound. "Is it true what they say about you? That you are strong and able to defeat the CCR?"

Cody looked at Rachel and raised one eyebrow. "What have you been telling these people about me?"

A light red flush crawled across Rachel's cheeks. "Nothing much. Are you through with that bowl?"

Cody handed it to her and winked at the boy. "Thanks for bringing my clothes. Now if you two will excuse me . . ."

He waited until he was alone and pulled his clothes on under the blanket. Then he threw back the hide and stood up. Walking was easy for him. He'd been practicing when no one was around. He walked across the floor and flexed his muscles. His shoulder was still incredibly sore but he could use it and he knew it was time to go.

"Looks like we are pretty good healers."

Cody turned around. Samuel was standing in the opening. "I brought you this." The tall man handed him a leather bridle. "I want you to have the pick of the horses we have cor-

ralled below. And don't forget your gun.
Rachel keeps it wrapped in that bag in the
corner."

"You knew I was leaving?"

"When Rachel told us of your mission, I assumed you would leave the instant you were
able."

"There is no way I can thank you enough
for all you've done—but I wonder if I could
ask one more thing."

"Of course."

"It's Rachel. She doesn't really understand
how rough it's going to be. . . ."

"And you want us to keep her here with
us?"

"Would you?"

Samuel nodded. "I'll go and tell the others
to keep her occupied for a while."

Cody extended his hand. "Thank you. If
I'm ever back this way, I'll be sure and look
you up."

"You will always be welcome."

Mike jumped on him and licked every part of his face. Cody hugged him with both arms. "I've missed you too."

The stocky dog barked as if he understood every word.

"They tell me you've been keeping an eye on my things down here. That's a good boy. Just as soon as I can catch one of these horses we'll load him up and be on our way. What do you say?"

Mike barked again and ran alongside Cody into the corral.

Cody shook out the bridle and tried for the nearest horse. It danced sideways, easily staying out of his reach.

"Something tells me this could be harder than it looks, boy. You wait outside. I think you're scaring them."

Mike obediently went to the edge of the fence and sat down. Cody shook out the bridle again and edged up to a large sorrel. He put his hand out and the horse snorted, whirled and kicked, narrowly missing him.

"Need some help with that?" Rachel called from behind him.

Cody's shoulders slumped. "What are you doing here?"

"I saw you trying to run out on me and I thought I'd follow along to see how far you could make it without my help. From here it doesn't look like you've gotten too far."

"I wasn't running out on you. It's better for you if you stay here."

"Listen, macho man. I'm a big girl and I'll decide what's best for me." Rachel stepped into the corral and took the bridle. "My parents used to run a horse farm, remember?"

Effortlessly she wrapped one end of a rein around the sorrel's neck. Then she slid the headstall over his face and fastened it. "Here." She held the reins out to Cody and then ducked under the bottom fence rail and ran back to the ladder. "You could have at least said goodbye."

Cody dropped the reins and trotted after her. "Rachel, wait." He took hold of her arm. "You're right. I shouldn't have just left like that. I'm sorry."

Rachel looked past him. "You're forgiven. And Cody . . . ?"

"Yeah?"

"I kind of got used to having you around." She looked away. "It would be awful if you got killed."

She moved quickly up the ladder and Cody watched her until she was out of sight and he thought, You've got that right, Rachel. It would be just awful.

Book Three

BREAKOUT

The blistering sun beat down on them without mercy. The hot air was thick and still and every breath was a struggle. There was no shade in sight, nothing but shimmering white sand for miles in any direction.

The horse stumbled and dropped, first to his knees and then all the way down. Cody stood facing him, tugging on the reins. "Come . . . on. Don't quit on me now."

Mike barked and nipped halfheartedly at

the horse's back feet but the exhausted animal wouldn't budge.

Cody stopped pulling. His arms ached and every movement was a strain. A trickle of salty sweat ran into his eyes. He didn't try to wipe it away. Instead, he slowly crawled to the horse and started unloading the canvas bags and boxes that were tied on its back.

When he finished, Cody lay down beside the horse to take advantage of what little shade its body offered. The dog joined him.

"I really got us into a jam this time, Mike." He ruffled the dog's ears. "Maybe what we need to do now is take a break. Just a short one . . ." He put his arm up to shield his eyes from the sun's fierce rays.

They had started across the sand more than two days earlier. Cody had hoped that this route would prove to be a shortcut to his destination in the desert.

But he'd been wrong. Now he was smack in the middle of seemingly endless dunes that led nowhere. Lying on the searing gypsum, he could feel his thoughts slowly slipping into delirium and he struggled to keep himself alert. Think, he chided himself. If you lose it now you're done for. Don't forget who you are and why you're here. There are people depending on you.

"I say we go ahead with our plans. Now that we have the guns and grenades we need . . ."

"No, Landers. They belong to the kid. As much as we need the stuff, we better wait and see what he was doing with them. Chances are he was carrying those things to someone who needs them a lot worse."

Landers spit on the ground in disgust. "Come on, Jake. What would a kid be doing with this kind of equipment unless he stole it?

He was probably on his way to sell it to the highest underground bidder. I say we take it."

The tall gray-headed man named Jake pulled the hood of his sand-colored poncho back and turned to look at the boy sleeping on the cot across the room. "If my hunch is right, that's no ordinary kid." He put his hand on Landers' shoulder. "Before we can do anything, we've got an army to train. Let's get to it."

Landers rolled his eyes and held the tent flap open. "Some army. A couple of old men and a handful of homeless kids."

Cody had listened to the entire exchange but thought it best not to let the men know he was awake until he was a little more sure of his surroundings.

After they left the tent he opened his eyes. He was lying on a hard cot inside a large off-white canvas tent. There were a desk and two chairs in one corner and a locked trunk near the back wall.

Carefully he rolled off the cot and crawled to the door. It was late afternoon. He could see that the camp was small and was set up on the edge of the sand near several trees and a small pool of water.

Outside he could hear the men barking orders. Cody moved away from the door. There was nothing here to tell him where he was or what kind of people had found him. His eyes fell on the trunk. He edged over to it and reached into his shirt pocket for the piece of wire he always carried.

Expertly he picked the lock and swung the lid open. Inside were maps, clothes and a picture of a tall man standing beside an F-119, the same kind of plane his dad had flown.

"Find anything in there that interests you?"

Cody spun around in a crouched position, his hands up ready to defend himself. The man in the picture was standing in the door with his arms folded.

"Not much." Cody straightened. "Where am I and why did you bring me here?"

The man unfolded his arms and moved to one of the chairs. "You are in the camp of what's left of G Company, United States Army. I'm Jake Christmas, Major. And I rescued you because you looked like you needed it. Now, you answer my questions. What's your name and what in Sam Hill are you doing out here alone carrying that small arsenal?"

Cody chose his words carefully. "My name is Cody, Cody Pierce. I'm on my way to . . . help some people out of a bad situation."

Jake sat quietly for a few seconds. He watched Cody warily. "I've seen the wanted posters on you. You're the White Fox. They say you escaped from one of their toughest prison camps and that you might be responsible for blowing up a weapons storage facility and killing the Republic guards who were stationed there."

"Don't believe everything you hear." Cody tried to act nonchalant. "Listen, I really appreciate your bringing me here. I would probably have died out there. Maybe sometime I can return the favor but now I need to be on my way." He paused. "Did my horse and dog make it?"

"Sorry, I had to put your horse down. He was all in. But your dog is fine. He's pretty

tough. One of the kids is taking care of him.
About returning that favor . . ."

Cody cocked his head suspiciously. "What
do you want?"

"Right now, if you feel up to it, I'd like you
to take a walk through camp with me. After
that, we'll discuss how you can pay me back."

CHAPTER 3

The bright sunlight made Cody squint. His eyes still burned from hours of staring at the glistening white sand.

His initial impression of the camp had been correct. It was on the fringe of a sand dune with only a handful of tents in a semicircle around a central compound.

Jake stopped on the edge of the grounds. A short stocky man with light brown hair cut in a flattop was standing in front of a group of kids, holding Cody's machine gun and explaining how it worked. They were all wearing lightweight sand-colored ponchos.

"Come on." Jake motioned for him to follow. "I want you to meet my . . . soldiers." He led Cody to the man who was doing the talking. "Captain Landers, meet Cody Pierce. Cody, this is Doug Landers, my next in command. And this"—he swung his hand around—"is all that's left of G Company."

Landers shook Cody's hand stiffly while the others crowded around.

The shortest boy, who Cody guessed couldn't be more than ten years old, weaseled his way in front of the others. A long black curl fell down on his forehead and he blew it off his face impatiently. "If you don't want your dog anymore I'll take him."

Cody raised an eyebrow. "I suspect that'll be up to him. Mike sort of goes where he wants."

Jake laughed. "This is Davey. He could talk the stripes off a zebra."

A tall African American boy stepped close. "How come you're so stupid you got caught out in the dunes?"

Cody squared his shoulders and stared

evenly at the boy. Finally a smile tugged at the corner of his mouth. "I guess it was kind of stupid, wasn't it?"

The boy relaxed and grinned. "I'm Damian but my friends call me Slick." He introduced the rest of the kids, pointing out each one in the circle. "This is Matt; he's so serious because his dad was a captain and he thinks that makes him regular army. Nick Trujillo is the pretty boy in back. The redhead is Trisha. She's the only girl in camp. And this hero is Patch." Slick stood behind a younger boy who wore a round brown patch over his left eye. Slick slapped him playfully on the back. "He got a little too close to an exploding grenade."

Cody smiled. So this was Jake's army. He thought back to when Colonel Wyman had told him that kids weren't really needed in this war. Cody gave them all a friendly glance. "Nice to meet you guys. And thanks for putting me up. I appreciate it."

"Well, I guess that's everybody," Jake said pleasantly, "except for the Smiths. If you're hungry we'll go to the mess tent and you can meet them. They do all the cooking, take care of the bees and generally look after everyone in the camp."

"Bees?" Cody looked at him curiously.

"It's a hobby of theirs. They started with a nest of wild ones. Now they have several hives. We don't mind because it keeps us in fresh honey."

Cody followed him to a tent with large screened windows. Three metal folding tables with benches sat in the middle and at one end hanging from a hook was the carcass of a large African oryx antelope. Eighty years before they had been planted on a missile range in New Mexico and now they were everywhere. Two elderly men were busy skinning it.

Cody stopped when he saw them. The men were identical. They were slight in build and their skin was brown and dry like overdone bacon. Their faces were lined and the crevices in them so deep it was hard to see the color of their eyes.

"Cody, this is Tom and Joe Smith. No one around here can ever tell them apart, so if you want one of them just holler 'Mr. Smith' and you'll get an answer."

"This the kid you found when you were out hunting?" one of the men asked.

Jake nodded.

"He stayin' for supper?" the other one questioned.

"He hasn't said yet." Jake turned to Cody. "Are you?"

"Am I invited?"

"Don't have to be invited around here." One of the twins started carving on the carcass again. "All you have to do is show up to the table."

"In that case," Cody said, rubbing his empty stomach, "I'm staying."

CHAPTER 4

"Have a chair, Cody. Captain Landers and I have a proposition for you."

Cody chewed his lip and settled down in one of the hard wooden chairs in Jake's tent.

Jake paced the floor twice and then stopped in front of him. "First let me tell you that just because I saved your life, your dog and your supplies—not to mention the fact that we fed you—I don't want you to feel obligated to do what we're about to ask."

Cody's eyes narrowed. "I'm not so sure I like where this is heading."

Jake grinned, then took a deep breath and ran his hand through his gray hair. "The captain and I need your help."

Landers cleared his throat. "And your weapons."

Cody shook his head. "I'd like to help you out but that stuff is earmarked. I have a private score to settle with the CCR."

"We could take it from you," Landers said irritably.

The chair Cody was sitting in creaked as he leaned back against the tent wall. He fixed Landers with a quiet look. "I can absolutely guarantee that you wouldn't have them long."

The tension in the room was thick. Landers started to say something, then let it die off.

Jake broke the silence. "We have no intention of stealing anything from you, Cody. We're all Americans here and we're all working for the good of what's left of our country. Captain Landers was out of line." He unfolded a large map and smoothed it out on the table. "Will you at least listen to what I have to say?"

"Sure." Cody let his chair drop. "I owe you that much."

"Here's our location." Jake pointed to a spot on the map. "The CCR doesn't know we're here yet. They never fly over because there's nothing out here in this desolate area they want. We're still careful, though—just in case."

"Is that why you wear those light-colored ponchos?" Cody asked.

"Right. They blend in with the sand." Jake pulled up the other chair. "This"—he pointed to a dark barbed line on the map—"is the Turbo Track. The CCR has been using it to transport supplies to outposts and camps in the desert."

"I've heard of it. When I was in the prison camp most of our supplies came off that train."

"So far the CCR has only used the Turbo for minor things like supplying the prison camps, so none of the U.S. resistance groups have bothered with it. But now we've received word that in two weeks' time a large shipment of raw trilithium is coming through."

"Whew." Cody's eyebrows went up. "The CCR must be building a few more nukes."

"They've taken over a nuclear laboratory in New Mexico. The shipment will be sent there on the Turbo."

"Okay, so what's the problem?" Cody shrugged. "Tell Colonel Wyman and the army to come over and take out the train."

"The problem is that we already sent this information to the higher-ups last month. But the first date we had was false. We took a squad out to stop the shipment and the CCR was waiting for us. The information was planted. They wanted to see what we would throw at them before they sent the real shipment." The creases in Jake's forehead deepened. "We lost most of the company. Those kids outside lost their parents on an empty run."

"I don't get it," Cody said, frowning. "Won't the army send you more troops for something this serious? Heck, they could do a hit-and-run in a chopper and put a stop to it."

"The word from headquarters is they don't have enough men to spare for something they're not absolutely sure of."

"Are *you* sure?" Cody asked thoughtfully.

"My source is the best there is—me. I can't tell you how I know. I just do."

"Do you have a plan?"

Jake sighed. "Not really. The kids are great but they don't know anything about fighting. Landers and I were going to have to use them anyway, at least as backup. I felt we had no other choice—that is, until now."

Cody ignored the last part of Jake's statement. "What did you have in mind?"

"The Turbo stops here to fuel up." Jake pointed to a black square on the map. "That's where we hit them the last time. But now we know they'll be ready for us. So Landers came up with the idea of waiting until they were on the way out of the fuel depot to attack. The train will be moving but not too fast."

"Good idea." Cody nodded. "Then you can target just the cars you want." He stood up and studied the map. "Right about here"— he tapped the map—"you could unhook a few of the cars and let the end of the train go. If there were any troops on them, they'd be stranded in the desert."

"Hmmm." Landers rubbed his chin. "Not a bad suggestion."

"The Smiths are our drivers," Jake cut in. "We were planning on having them meet us here, outside Tingley, where we'll offload and then bring the stuff back to camp until headquarters tells us what to do with it."

Cody walked around the table and studied the map. "I could be wrong, Major. But I think you and I might be able to work something out. According to this map the Turbo can be rerouted to another track that comes pretty close to the place I was headed anyway. If G Company is willing to alter its plans a little, I just might be able to help you guys out."

CHAPTER 5

"All right, G Company, listen up." Jake clapped his hands and the young people gathered around him. "Cody has agreed to lend us some of his weapons and explosives along with his expertise so that we can go ahead with our mission as scheduled. For the next week and a half he will be helping Captain Landers and myself with your training. You will obey his orders just the way you would mine. Is that understood?"

"Yes, sir," they barked in unison.

"Okay, Cody." Jake winked at him. "You're on."

Cody blew air through his teeth and stepped forward. "I'm not going to pretend to be an expert on everything but thanks to some good friends of mine I do know how to use these guns and how to fight a little. We don't have a lot of time so I'm going to concentrate on what I think will help us the most. Everybody line up facing me." Cody started them on hand-to-hand combat.

Jake and Landers backed out of the way. "That kid is a natural-born leader," Jake whispered.

"We'll see," Landers replied skeptically.

"No. Not like that, Davey. You're small, so you can't try to take them with strength. You have to come in mean and hit 'em where it counts. Try it again."

Jake smiled. "He's already got them thinking they can pull this off. That's more than we did."

"They're just kids, Jake. How are they

going to take on grown men? I've never liked the idea of using them. You and I should do it alone."

"We'd never get it done, Doug. You know that. Look what happened the last time."

Cody gave Trisha a hand up off the ground where he'd thrown her. "Rule number one. If you're going to attack somebody, do it like you mean it or stay home. These guys won't be playing around. I spent eighteen months with them and I know. Good intentions don't count. They'll kill you just the same. Now come at me again."

CHAPTER 6

Cody gave Mike a big piece of scrap meat the Smiths had saved for him and Mike sat up and begged for more.

"I know what a big hog you are, so I brought you this." Cody took out of his shirt a biscuit dripping with fresh honey, wrapped in paper. "Here, try this. The bees worked overtime."

Davey and Patch stopped playing checkers and watched Cody play and wrestle with Mike. "Where'd you get him?" Davey asked. "He's a great dog."

"He belonged to a friend of mine who got himself killed. After that Mike sort of adopted me."

"Is it true what the others are saying about you?" Patch asked. "That you're the White Fox?"

"Where did you hear that?" Cody reached down and stroked Mike's head.

"From Matt, mainly. He says he saw a flyer on you when he and his dad left their home in East Texas and came west to join G Company. He says there's a big reward on you. Is it true?"

"Why? You thinking about collecting it?"

Patch made a face. "Heck no. I was just wondering. You know, what it was like to be in one of those camps for so long."

"Why don't you squirts leave him alone?" Trisha moved down the aisle. "He probably doesn't want to talk about it."

Cody smiled up at her. "I was kinda rough on you today. Are you okay?"

Trisha's green eyes flashed. She flipped her long red braid behind her back. "I can take it. Don't worry about me."

"I wasn't worried. I was just asking."

Nick, Matt and Slick tramped through the door. Nick moaned and fell on his bed, resting his sand-covered head on a makeshift pillow. "Wake me up when the war's over."

Matt's freckled face slipped into a frown. He took off his poncho. "Technically that might take years. Considering the advantage the CCR has at this point, you could be an old man by the time—"

"Give it a rest, buzz brain." Slick threw a boot at him. "Nick didn't mean it like that. He was just whining."

"Whining?" Nick sat up on his elbows. "If I wasn't dog tired I'd show you who's whining."

"Anytime, pretty boy."

Cody watched them without saying anything. It was obvious that these guys were good friends. He felt a twinge of jealousy. He'd never had any friends his own age. Luther, Franklin and even Rico had all been older and they'd made him feel as if he were older too. Well, there was Rachel. He guessed Rachel was a friend. Or something.

A voice broke into his thoughts. "Isn't that right, slave driver?"

"What?" Cody blinked. "Sorry, I wasn't listening."

Trisha folded her arms. "I was telling these idiots that you probably had a killer day planned for us tomorrow and they better quit goofing and get some sleep."

"Uh, right. We've still got a lot of ground to cover before we try to take that train."

Nick moaned. "Why me?"

"If I recall," Matt explained, "you volunteered for this mission because you wanted to take your father's place. The major didn't really choose you at all. He only . . ."

Slick groaned and turned out the light.

CHAPTER 7

"You're doing a lot better, Nick. If that sand-bag had been alive before you started shooting, it'd be dead now." Cody looked down the row. Patch was having trouble loading a small submachine gun.

"I think it's jammed, Cody."

"Be careful where you point that thing." Cody moved over to him. "Let me take a look."

"I'll do that." Landers walked briskly toward the line. "The major wants to see you in his quarters."

Cody nodded and trotted across the grounds to Jake's tent. The flap was open, so he put his head through. "You wanted to see me?"

"Yeah. There are a couple of last-minute details we need to go over. Come on in."

"What's up?" Cody ducked inside.

"I've just received word that the CCR is worried. They're beefing up defenses on the Turbo. They've called in a security advisor. Some clown named Gollgath. Ever heard of him?"

Cody's jaws tightened. "I've heard of him. He's a very dangerous man. And he's smart. He'll have all the angles figured."

"Should we call it off?"

A picture of the dead soldiers at the warehouse flooded into Cody's mind. His lips twisted with bitterness. "No, Major. This is one mission we better do everything we can to accomplish. Gollgath is an animal with rabies. Crazy mean."

"Watch yourself, Cody. Don't let emotions cloud your judgment."

"Is there anything else?"

"Yes . . ." Jake hesitated. "There is. Landers has been against involving the kids in this thing from the start. He's asked me to at least consider letting Patch and Davey stay with the Smiths. What do you think?"

Cody rubbed the back of his neck. "That's a tough call. If they get hurt, you'll feel responsible. On the other hand, everybody out on those grounds thinks of this mission as a way to avenge their parents' deaths. I'm not sure it would be fair for you to take that away from them."

"So you'd let them go?"

"I didn't say that. I said it wouldn't be fair to take away what might be their only chance to get back at the CCR. If I were in charge, I think I'd make it clear to everyone that the Smiths are getting up there in years and that their part of the mission, securing the shipment, is the most important. After we take it, it has to be protected by someone who knows what they're doing. If it isn't, we might as well have left it on the train."

"You know," Jake said with a laugh, "you have a gift for coming up with solutions. When this is all over I think I'll put you in for a promotion."

"You forget," Cody said dryly, "I'm not in the army."

"That's a matter of opinion, soldier." Jake turned back to his work. "A matter of opinion."

CHAPTER 8

"Think this'll work?" Slick threw a shovelful of dirt out of the trench he and Cody were digging.

"It better." Cody leaned on the handle of his shovel. He could barely see the roof of the train depot. "Gollgath will figure the army will definitely try something. Our advantage is that he doesn't know when, how or where. When the Turbo stops at the depot tomorrow, he'll have troops out scouring the area looking for any sign of a problem."

Matt and Nick set the last of Cody's supplies by the ditch. "What's in this black bag?" Nick asked.

"That's a surprise package I put together for Gollgath." Cody started shoveling again. "Are Trisha and Landers through covering the tracks the Smiths made getting us here?"

Matt shook his head. "They're not back yet. But don't worry. Landers is a perfectionist. The CCR won't be able to tell a bug crossed the road when he's through."

"Okay, you and Nick better start tearing these crates apart to make the covers for our trenches. When Jake gets back from scouting out the depot he'll expect us to have things about finished out here."

"Here he comes now," Matt said, squinting. "He sure can run for an old man."

Cody whipped around. Jake was low and running at full steam. "Something's wrong," Cody said, jumping out of the trench and grabbing his submachine gun.

"We got . . . problems, boys." Jake gasped for breath. "A . . . CCR patrol found Landers and Trisha. Landers is dead. They took

Trisha. . . . They're at the depot now. My guess is . . . they'll take her to that prison camp Cody told us about for questioning."

Nick shouldered his gun. "What are we waiting for? Let's go get her."

"Not so fast." Jake took a swig of water from his canteen. "If we go blasting in there now our chances of stopping the train tomorrow are zero."

Nick exploded. "Are you saying we're just going to leave her?"

"We don't have any choice." Jake wiped the sweat off his forehead. "If they find out we're here, it's all over."

"Jake's right, Nick," Slick said softly. "Trisha's tough. She can hold out till after we take the train."

Cody held his tongue. He knew firsthand what Sidoron did to prisoners who refused to talk. The thought of Trisha in his hands made Cody cringe. They would probably never see her alive again. He swallowed hard. "Jake's calling the shots. We better get back to work or we won't be ready when the Turbo comes through."

CHAPTER 9

Cody coughed. He felt as if he'd been sealed in his own coffin. Jake had waited until the last minute before the Turbo was due to order them into the board- and sand-covered trenches. Jake had checked to make sure they'd left no telltale signs before he crawled into his own space.

There was nothing to do now but wait. It was impossible to get comfortable. The trenches weren't very big and their bodies were draped with guns and grenades.

Cody's area was particularly small because he'd insisted on bringing a few extra items—like the black bag.

He resisted the urge to enlarge his airhole and tried to take slow shallow breaths.

From somewhere nearby he could hear voices speaking in the Republic language. He'd been right when he had predicted Gollgath would deploy CCR scouts to check out the area.

The sound of boots crunching on the crusty sand made Cody freeze. Someone was walking around above them.

A loud horn blasted from the depot and he heard running footsteps. The soldiers were leaving, hurrying back to board the train.

Jake pushed up on the planks covering his part of the trench until he could see the terrain in front of him. The area appeared to be clear. The Turbo blew its whistle again and started inching down the track toward them.

"Okay, boys," Jake mumbled, "time for a little train ride."

All the lumber came off and G Company

scrambled out of the trenches into the sunlight.

Following Jake's lead, the four boys pulled
the hoods of their ponchos up and wormed
across the sand on their stomachs until they
were lying close to the tracks.

The Turbo was picking up speed. The engine passed and then several of the cars.

Jake waited until all that was left were the
four flatcars on the end. He sprang to his feet
and broke into a run. "Let's go. It's now or
never."

The five of them charged the train, grabbing anything they could find to hang on to.
Jake and Slick landed on the second flatcar
and immediately assumed a prone position in
case the CCR happened to spot them.

Cody and Nick hit the third car. Nick did
a belly-flop and lay there for a few moments
with the wind knocked out of him.

Matt was having trouble. He ran alongside
the third car but couldn't quite overtake it.
The fourth car was getting away from him
too. He made a wild grab for the short ladder
at the very end.

He caught it. The train jerked him a few steps, almost breaking his hold. He jumped, barely landing on the bottom step.

Jake was already on his feet, moving down the row of cars. He didn't look back. Each person had a job to do and his was to take over the engine.

Matt's was to unhook the coupling on the passenger cars so that they could leave most of the troops behind them, and then to climb on top as a lookout.

Slick was supposed to find the radio room and put the communications officer out of commission so that the soldiers couldn't contact help. And Cody and Nick had to locate the special shipment and persuade Gollgath and his guards to hand it over.

One by one they climbed up the ladder to the roof of the first passenger car, moving carefully across the top and down the other side.

Near the front of the second troop car Jake held up his hand. He gestured toward something below him.

A soldier had stepped out of the car to smoke a cigarette.

Jake slipped his knife out of his boot, grabbed hold of a vent pipe and swung down. In seconds they saw his hand motioning for them to continue. Cody noticed a smear of dark red blood on the railing as they passed. He moved on quickly.

Jake and Slick kept moving toward the front of the train. Matt had already dropped off at the last troop car. Nick and Cody were kneeling on the top of one of the freight cars.

Nick pointed down and Cody shrugged. He had no way of knowing for sure which of the two freight cars held the trilithium and its armed guard.

He waited the three minutes Jake had said to give him before taking off his shoulder the laser gun he'd stolen from the warehouse. He adjusted the ray to a fine line and fired. The thick steel in the top of the car melted like butter, creating an opening the size of a man-hole cover.

When the smoke cleared, Cody helped lower Nick into the car and then dropped through himself.

"This isn't it," Nick said. "It must be in the

next car. These crates have pictures of food and baby formula on them."

"Wait. Something's not right." Cody stared at the boxes.

"Come on, Pierce. We don't have much time."

"Give me a minute." Cody took his combat knife out of his boot and pried open one edge of a large crate.

"What are you doing, Cody? This can't be it. Jake said the shipment would be heavily guarded."

"Jake doesn't know Gollgath." Cody pulled a lead container the size of a shoebox out of the crate.

It was locked. He reached inside his poncho for his piece of wire and had the box open in seconds.

"Well, what do you know?" Nick gaped at the large pieces of crystal ore inside. "Gollgath thought he could fool us by not placing a guard in the car and by putting fake labels on the crates. How did you know it was a trick?"

Cody closed the lid on the box and put it

back in the crate. "The CCR could care less about feeding American babies. They kill every one they find. It doesn't make sense that they would go to the trouble of transporting milk for them."

"Come on, genius. Let's go see how the rest of them are making out." Nick offered Cody a leg up.

When Cody was out he reached down and pulled Nick up. Matt was sitting on top, grinning. He pointed behind him.

Half the train had been left at a standstill behind them.

Cody slapped him on the shoulder. "Good job. Any sign of trouble up front?"

Matt shook his head.

"Good." Cody moved to the front of the car. "I'll be right back. I've got a little present for an old friend of mine."

He jumped to the roof of the next freight car and took the black bag off his shoulder. This car, like the last one, was fitted with an old-fashioned air-conditioning unit on the top. Cody snapped off the cover and unzipped his bag. Then he quickly dumped the contents inside and closed the lid.

It didn't take long to see results. The door of the freight car flew open and three soldiers covered with wild bees screamed as they leaped off the fast-moving train.

Someone fired shots at them from inside.

Cody waited. There was no sign of Gollgath. He lay down on his stomach and leaned over the edge of the car to get a better look.

Slumped in the corner of the car was the bald CCR officer, completely covered with hundreds of angry stinging bees.

Cody studied the man, seeing no movement, no breathing. He sighed. Must have been allergic to beestings, he thought. Probably the first few killed him. Cody fought his disappointment—he had wanted it to be slower.

CHAPTER 10

The train squealed to a grinding halt outside the ghost town of Tingley. Jake immediately made his way back to the other cars to check on the boys.

Slick was waiting for him in the radio room. "Hello, Major," he said weakly. "Mission accomplished."

Jake saw the blood on Slick's sleeve and pants leg. "What happened?"

"Nothing that won't heal. There were two of them. I told them to get off. One did but the other one had a knife. He turned on me and knocked my gun out of my hands. Tell Cody his training sure came in handy. I rammed the guy with my head and pushed him out the door."

"Not before he took a couple of pieces out of you. Let me have a look at that." Jake gently helped Slick out of his poncho and shirt.

"Some people will do anything for a little attention." Cody stood in the door. "How bad is it?"

"It's bad," Jake answered. "I'll wrap it up the best I can and when the Smiths get here we'll send him back with them. How are the others?"

Cody set his gun down. "Nick and Matt are fine. We found the car with the shipment. They had it disguised."

"What about Gollgath?" Jake asked.

"He's out of the picture for good."

"Oh."

Two large transport trucks in camouflage paint pulled alongside the train. Cody grabbed his gun. "I'll help the others load the crates. You stay with Slick."

Cody directed the Smiths to back up as close as possible to the door of the freight car. Patch and Davey stepped from the bed of the truck into the train.

"Where is everybody?" Davey asked.

"We ran into some trouble." Nick frowned. "Landers is dead and the CCR got Trisha. But don't worry, we're going after her just as soon as we get this stuff loaded."

"And Slick got cut up some." Cody started sliding one of the crates toward the door. "Jake's in the radio room taking care of him. He'll be going back to camp with you."

"I wish I didn't have to protect this shipment," Patch said sulkily. "I'd go with you and take Slick's place."

"I know you would." Cody waited for the second truck to move into position. "But this time you better follow orders. We don't want to have to tell Trisha that it was all for nothing, do we?"

Patch shook his head.

"Did you guys bring the stuff I asked for?" Cody glanced in the bed of the truck.

"It's all here, including the grenade launcher. Davey and I will unload it for you."

When the vehicles were ready, Cody helped Jake carry Slick to the front seat of the second truck and set him inside.

"You guys don't have too much fun without me, okay?" Slick smiled feebly.

"We'll try not to." Jake pounded the roof of the truck. "Get going. Take the route we talked about and be careful."

The trucks left in a cloud of dust.

"Let's move," Jake ordered. "Nick and I will run the engine. Cody, since you speak their language, you and Matt take the radio room. Go ahead and make that call to your chopper pilot friend and then monitor the Turbo's frequency. Pay attention to what they say but watch how you answer. We've only got a couple of hours before that shipment is due. After that they'll come looking. Any questions?"

Three tired young soldiers shook their heads.

"All right then. Take your positions and we'll head this train south."

CHAPTER 11

They were sitting on a side rail near the bombed-out town of Spanish Wells. A transmission came over the radio.

"What'd they say?" Matt whispered.

"Shhh." Cody held his finger to his lips and kept listening. When they were through, Cody took the mike and answered them in the Republic language.

"Well?" Matt questioned. "Are you going to tell me what's going on?"

"That was the radio operator at the main

station. He was just checking to see if we were on schedule. And since we are right on the money as far as our timetable is concerned, I answered him in the affirmative."

Matt smiled. "When this is all over maybe you could teach me how to talk—" He looked out the window. Two vehicles were approaching the train. "Uh-oh. Grab your gun. That first jeep has a Republic symbol painted on the side."

Cody shouldered his laser gun and quietly slipped out the back door with Matt on his heels. They climbed down and edged around the side of the train.

A Republic soldier was driving the jeep and a woman dressed in civilian clothes was at the wheel of the truck. The soldier stepped out and walked toward the train.

"Hold it right there," Cody ordered. "Tell your partner to get out of the truck."

The young corporal turned and shouted instructions to his comrade. The tall woman stepped out and waited.

From the engine Jake heard the commotion and came running. He stopped when he saw the soldier. "So you've finally been captured, Yuri. It's about time."

"That's not funny, Jake. Tell your men to put down their guns. I'm on your side, remember?"

"It's all right, Cody. This is Yuri, my contact. He brought us some transportation."

Cody stepped out in the open and lowered his gun barrel. "Sorry about that. It's the uniform. I get sorta nervous every time I see one."

"No hard feelings." Yuri handed Jake the keys to the jeep. "I better get back before they wonder where I am."

"Thanks. I'll be in touch." Jake shook hands and the soldier hopped into the truck with the woman and drove away.

Jake turned to Cody. "Well, you've had a long wait but it's finally time. Your problems are now our problems. Let's go visit your prison camp."

Jake started the Turbo's engine and set the acceleration lever on top speed—in reverse.

He jumped down and watched the giant silver machine pick up momentum. "When this end smashes into the cars Matt left stranded on the tracks it should make quite a mess. Maybe it'll give the CCR something to think about so they won't have time to worry about us."

"How far is the prison camp from here?" Nick asked.

"It'll take a few hours of hard driving." Jake turned to Cody. "Did you make that call to your pilot friend?"

"It took a bit to get her—she hadn't heard from me in so long she thought I was dead. But Toni said she'll be watching for our signal."

"I guess that's it, then." Jake let out a deep breath. "The rest is up to us." He climbed into the driver's side of the jeep and waited for the others to find room around Cody's arsenal.

They drove at breakneck speed across the open desert through the greasewood and yuccas. An hour away from the tracks Cody noticed a cloud of dust coming toward them. He looked through his binoculars.

"It's a patrol, Jake."

Jake glanced around, looking for cover. There wasn't much. He whipped the utility vehicle into a shallow gully and ordered everyone to spread out.

Cody reset his laser gun for a bigger target and waited.

Three Republic trucks were coming straight for them. Cody took a bead on the first one and fired. The truck was instantly incinerated, melted to a puddle. Quickly he took aim at the second one. The soldiers inside leaped clear just before he fired.

The third driver threw on his brakes and the troops in the back dove off the sides, shooting wildly at everything in sight. Matt and Nick returned their fire, making them run for cover.

Cody aimed and the last truck disappeared.

"Everybody back in the rig," Jake ordered. He fired a barrage of bullets to keep the soldiers busy as G Company made its way down the gully.

Keeping low, Cody crawled into the driver's side and started the engine. Matt dove into the back and Nick landed on top of him. Jake ran backward to the door, shooting as he came.

When Jake jumped in, Cody mashed the gas pedal to the floor. A hailstorm of bullets chased them as they plowed down the sandy gully and out the other side.

"Whew." Jake wiped his forehead with his sleeve. "That was close."

"I think we're getting good at this line of work, Major." Matt pushed Nick off him. "Either that or it's just our lucky day."

"Luck is great," the major said softly. "Just don't count on it."

CHAPTER 13

Cody drew a picture in the dirt of the prison camp layout. "The main gate is here. There are two lookout towers on either side with armed guards. They have orders to shoot first and ask questions later. There will also be guards at the gate."

"Where will they be holding Trisha?" Matt asked.

Cody hesitated. "You guys should know that the chances of Trisha's still being alive are pretty slim. When Sidoron gets a prisoner he needs information from he doesn't care what he has to do to get it."

Nick frowned. "You didn't mention anything about his earlier—"

"It's not Cody's fault Trisha was captured," Jake interrupted. "If she's alive we'll get her out. For now let's stick to business. We've got to learn where everything is in the camp while we still have daylight." He looked at Cody. "Where do they keep the prisoners?"

"In these barracks." Cody tapped a spot on the dirt with his stick. "The one on the end is where the kids stay. The rest are adults. Prisoners like Trisha and anyone else the CCR considers useful are put in cages in the ground behind the main headquarters until they're finally shot or beaten to death. That's where they'll take me."

"What's he talking about, Major?" Matt asked. "Why would the CCR take Cody anywhere?"

Jake scratched his head uncomfortably. "Well . . . it was Cody's idea. He believes the best way to get into the camp is right through the front gate. I'm taking him in as a way to gain favor."

CHAPTER 14

"Are you sure you're ready for this?" Jake slowed the jeep. "We could always try to find some other way."

"This is the best way and we both know it." Cody looked down the road at the tall barbed-wire fences. "I just hope we can pull it off. You better step on it before the tower guards get suspicious."

Jake nodded grimly and picked up speed until he pulled to a stop a few yards from the front gate.

A stone-faced guard stepped in front of them and shouted in an impatient voice, "Halt. State your business."

"I'm a loyalist and I have a prisoner for Colonel Sidoron," Jake yelled back. "The White Fox."

The guard cautiously stepped closer and inspected the back of the jeep and looked underneath. A second guard stood ready with his rifle, watching, and he smiled tightly when he recognized Cody. "So, you're back."

Cody said nothing.

When the first guard finished his inspection, he stood up and waved to the tower. Then he turned to Jake. "You may enter but you must leave your weapons here."

Jake wore Cody's laser gun on his shoulder and his finger was on the trigger of the submachine gun in his lap. Plastic explosives that the guard couldn't detect were hidden under his clothes.

"I don't think so, Sergeant. I haven't survived this long making stupid moves. If Sidoron doesn't want my little prize, I'll take him somewhere else. It doesn't matter to me as long as I get the credit. I'll be famous either way."

"Wait here." The guard whispered something to his comrade and opened the gate. He climbed into the back of the jeep. "You may proceed."

Cody fought to control his feelings as they drove down the dirt road. Everything looked the same as it had the day he and Toni had escaped. He could almost see Luther's body hanging from the fence. There were no prisoners in sight but he knew that was because they had to be on their bunks before dark or suffer the consequences.

The jeep stopped in front of the camp commander's office. Jake stepped out and roughly pulled Cody from the passenger side.

Cody's hands were tied in front of him and the ropes were burning into his wrists. He had insisted that Jake make it look authentic; otherwise, Sidoron wouldn't be fooled.

The guard ran up the wooden steps and inside the double doors. In moments the doors burst open and Sidoron strode onto the porch.

Cody stared up at him.

The commander took the steps slowly until he finally stood before them. Without warning he struck Cody across the side of the face.

Cody's knees buckled from the force of the blow but he managed to stay on his feet.

Sidoron circled behind him and grabbed a handful of Cody's hair. He jerked the youth's head back and held a long sharp knife to his throat.

"Hold it right there," Jake demanded. "No damaging the goods until I get my money."

Sidoron noticed the major for the first time. He reluctantly lowered the knife. "How dare you speak to me like that? Has no one ever taught you how to address your superiors?"

"I don't know about that. All I know is you offered a reward on this kid and I want it. He wasn't exactly easy to catch. I don't want to kill him until I get credit from the proper authorities for his capture."

"Shoot this man," Sidoron ordered.

The guard leveled his rifle at Jake's head.

"I wouldn't do that if I were you," Jake drawled.

"And why is that?" Sidoron's eyes narrowed to tiny yellow slits.

Jake opened the palm of his hand and revealed a round metal object. "Ever see one of these before, Colonel? It's a photon detonator. All it takes is one tiny little push on this button and this whole camp will blow sky-high."

"Disregard that order, Sergeant." Sidoron moved around Cody and stood on the bottom step studying Jake. "I like you, bounty hunter. You have a good head on your shoulders."

"Do we have a deal, then?" Jake asked.

Sidoron smiled. A quick flash of teeth; then the smile was gone. "Of course we do. Unfortunately it may take some time to collect your money. I'll have to wire headquarters."

"How long will that take?"

"Three, perhaps four days. These things must go through channels. In the meantime, may we offer you some of the comforts of our humble camp?"

"What comforts would they be?"

"What is your name?"

"Christmas. Jake Christmas. Remember that name, Colonel. You'll be hearing it again."

"Guard, take Mr. Christmas to the VIP guest quarters and see to it that he is made comfortable. And under no circumstance is he to be left alone."

Jake hesitated. "What are you going to do with the kid?"

Sidoron licked his puffy lips. "Don't worry about him, Mr. Christmas. The White Fox and I are old friends. We have a lot of catching up to do."

CHAPTER 15

The bright light in the interrogation room attracted a variety of insects. Cody sat with his hands still tied, watching them, wondering if he'd been like the moths that persisted in flying too close to the bulb until finally they touched the hot glass and killed themselves.

Footsteps sounded in the hall. When the door opened, Cody knew who it was without looking.

Sidoron was carrying a black swagger stick.

He moved his large frame behind the small desk and sat down.

"How have you been, White Fox?"

Cody was silent.

"Come now. We're not going to get anywhere like this. If I remember correctly, you escaped before I had a chance to show you how easily I am able to convince people of their need to talk." He reached over the desk and slapped Cody across the cheek with the stick, leaving an ugly red welt. "You made me a laughingstock. I lost an important promotion because of you."

Cody studied the colonel through cold gray eyes. Sidoron had grown flabby eating the best foods and sitting behind a desk all day. With the martial arts Rico had taught Cody at the warehouse, he knew he could take him even with his hands tied.

But it wasn't time.

"What are you thinking, White Fox? I can tell you've changed considerably since you were here. You have a different look about you and you don't seem afraid of me anymore. What kinds of things have you been doing?

We've heard stories, of course, but why don't you tell us which ones are true?"

Silence.

"When you escaped with your friend Major McLaughlin, where did she take you? Did you go to the rebel base?" Sidoron paused. "I need to know the location of that base. It would restore the confidence my superior officers once had in me."

He walked around the desk. "Still don't want to talk to me? What a pity, seeing that we are such old friends. No matter."

Sidoron took his combat knife out of its scabbard and started cleaning his fingernails. "Before I'm through with you, White Fox, you'll beg to speak to me."

He moved to the door and yelled for the guards.

Two husky soldiers marched in and pulled him off the chair. They dragged him to a corner of the room where a long rope was hanging from the ceiling. Then they tied it to the cord around his hands and hoisted him off the floor.

One of the guards took a rubber hose off a

shelf and swung, striking Cody viciously across the ribs.

Instinctively Cody drew both feet up and kicked. His boots took the man full in the face and he fell back, holding his broken nose.

Sidoron laughed. "See, I was right. You have changed, White Fox. Too bad you chose not to become one of us. We could have used you. As it is . . ." He motioned to the second guard. "Show him we're serious. Extremely serious."

The guard picked up a coiled whip and shook it out.

CHAPTER 16

It was midnight. Jake opened the door of his room and peered out. The guard Sidoron had stationed outside the guest quarters was snoring.

Jake tiptoed past him and out the side door. The searchlight from the tower was sweeping the grounds. He flattened himself against the wall until the light moved away.

The instant it was gone he darted across to the main building and slipped inside. Cody had told him that Sidoron would be holding him either in one of the cages or in the interrogation room.

Jake crept down the long corridor and pushed the door open. Cody was still hanging from the ceiling. His back was raw and bloody and he was either unconscious . . . or dead.

The major grabbed the nearest chair and stood on it to cut the rope. Cody fell into his arms.

"I knew this was a bad idea. Why did I ever listen to you?" He helped Cody sit up. "Wake up, kid. You gotta be okay."

One eye opened and then the other. Cody's voice was low, strained. "What makes you think I'm not okay, Major?"

"You're all right?"

Cody flexed his sore shoulders and rubbed his aching wrists. "It's a trick I learned from Toni. Let them beat on you a while. Then make them think you're a lot worse off than you are and they'll leave you alone. They thought I was so bad off they didn't even leave a guard."

"Your back looks pretty rough. Are you

going to be able to pull off your part of the mission?"

"I didn't come this far to quit now."

Jake handed Cody his laser gun. "Let's do it."

Cody led the way down the hall to the back of the building. "The cages are back here," he whispered. "The moon's out. We should be able to see fairly well."

They quietly made their way down the steps to the group of cells buried in the ground. Cody checked the first one. It was empty. A low moan came from the cell on the end.

"Trisha," Jake called softly. "Are you here?"

Cody took his piece of wire from inside his boot, scooted to the other side and picked the lock on the cage door.

At the bottom of the filthy hole huddled in the corner was a mass of tangled red hair.

"Trisha." Jake jumped down. "We've come to take you out of here."

The hair moved and Trisha looked up. She was barely recognizable. Her face was swollen and purple and some of her teeth were missing. "Is it . . . really you or am I dreaming?"

"It's me. We have to hurry. Give Cody your hand."

Trisha tried to stand and fell back against the cell wall.

"They've beat her up bad, Cody. I'm going to lift her out."

Jake sat her on the edge of the hole and pulled himself out beside her. "I've got some explosives to set. You go with Cody and he'll get you to safety. Can you do it?"

Trisha nodded, her voice hardly audible. "I guess I have to."

Jake disappeared into the darkness and Cody helped Trisha to her feet. They hobbled to the bushes near the next building and waited for the searchlight to sweep across.

"We're going to have to move fast now, Trisha. Ready?"

"I'm ready."

Cody put his arm around her waist and half pulled her across the open compound to the back of the children's barracks. He was breathing hard. "Wait here. I'll be right back."

Sliding under the barracks, he made his way to the opening in the floor he'd made when he was an inmate. He pushed up on it, laid it aside and wriggled through, surprised no one had ever found the hole.

In the dim light he walked down the row of beds to one special cot and sat down. Gently he shook the sleepy-eyed five-year-old girl awake.

"Cody!" She wrapped her arms around him. "Oh, Cody. You said you'd come back for me. It's been so long I thought you forgot me."

There was a stir among the other kids. Soon everyone was awake. When they saw Cody they rushed to his side.

He held his finger to his lips. "Everybody listen. We're getting out of here. I want you to stay together and do what I tell you. No questions."

Cody took them to the opening and dropped through. One by one they followed him. He edged out from under the barracks and sat next to Trisha. "Keep an eye on these guys, will you? If the shooting starts before I get back, head for the fence. Matt and Nick should have it cut by now."

The next barracks would be harder. Cody wasn't sure if any of the adults would remember him. He waited for the light to fade away and then slipped through the door. At the first cot he came to, he put his hand on the sleeping man's shoulder and shook him.

"What?" The man sat up. "Who are you? What are you doing here?"

"I'm . . . the White Fox. I've come to help you escape. Wake up the rest of the men and hide under the building. Send someone to spread the word to the other barracks. When the shooting starts, everybody head for the east fence as fast as you can. There'll be someone waiting there to meet you and help get you out."

"Cody." An older man who used to peel potatoes when Cody worked in the kitchen sat up on his cot. "It's good to see you, son. You're quite a hero around here."

"Good to see you too, Herman. Now get everybody up and hurry. Time's running out."

Cody cracked the door to check the location of the searchlight and then quickly dove underneath the barracks.

What he intended to do next he had deliberately withheld from Jake. Their plan had been for Jake to set the necessary explosives and meet Cody along with the inmates at the east fence, where Nick and Matt would be waiting and watching.

Cody had known all along that it couldn't end like that. He still had one piece of unfinished business—Sidoron.

The open compound was the most dangerous place to be and Cody had to time his move perfectly. The instant the light moved in a different direction he ran full blast toward the main building and slid to a stop, hiding in the shadows.

Sidoron's private quarters were next to his office. Cody knew them well because he had delivered the colonel's meals there every day for more than a year.

He opened the door and silently crept in. The guard was asleep in a chair outside the office. Cody stole up beside him and landed a brutal karate chop on the side of his neck. The guard slumped over and fell to the floor.

The office door was locked. Cody had known it would be. He took his piece of wire, jiggled it inside the keyhole and turned the knob.

It was dark in the office and Cody stumbled over a chair, sending it crashing across the room.

"Behren, is that you?"

Cody leaped to his feet and burst into Sidoron's bedroom with his laser gun leveled in front of him.

"Surprise, Colonel."

Sidoron hastily pulled the black sleeping mask off his face. "White Fox! How did you—"

"Keep your voice down, Colonel. We don't want to wake anybody."

"You'll never get away with this."

"Away with what, Colonel? What do you think I should do with you? Maybe you'd like to try a little of the rubber hose treatment, or we could go get the whip your goons used on me. I know, maybe I'll take my knife and skin you alive."

"Don't be too hasty, White Fox. I'm a powerful man. I have the ability to make you rich."

"Really? How much is your murdering scumbag life worth these days, Sidoron? A hundred thousand? Two hundred thousand?"

"Whatever you want. Just name it."

"I want my friend Luther Swift back from the dead and all the others you tortured and killed." Cody gestured with the laser gun. "Get out of bed."

Sidoron threw back the covers and stood on the wooden floor in a long white nightshirt, his feet bare.

Cody backed up and set his gun on the floor. "How tough are you when you have to do your own fighting, Sidoron?"

"You will find I am tough enough. You are a fool, White Fox." Sidoron lunged at him. Cody ducked, brought his right leg up and landed a solid kick to the man's jaw. The colonel staggered backward, regained his balance and swung, hitting Cody in the shoulder.

Before Sidoron could swing again, Cody hit him twice in the stomach, jumped and smashed his feet into the man's chest.

The colonel wobbled and gasped for breath.

"You're nothing, Sidoron. I could easily kill you with my bare hands." Cody picked up his gun in disgust. "Instead I think I'll do worse. I'm going to humiliate you to the point that you'll be lucky if the CCR will allow you to dig ditches for them. Let's go for a little walk."

An explosion rocked the building. Cody poked Sidoron in the ribs with his gun. "Don't worry about a thing, Colonel. That's just the sound of your kingdom crashing down around you. The guard towers probably aren't there anymore."

He pushed the portly man down the hall to the back door. Sidoron turned and pleaded, "You don't have to do this, White Fox. Think about it. I could set you up in the black market. We could be partners. There is no limit to what we could make together."

Cody laughed, a low chuckle with no humor in it. "I'd rather be partners with a rattlesnake. Open the door."

Outside they could hear machine-gun fire and more explosions. Cody ignored them.

"Get in the cage, Colonel. The one on the end. You'll find it open."

Sidoron crawled down into the same hole they had found Trisha in earlier. Cody secured the iron grate on top and locked it. "Now hand up your clothes."

"This is an outrage."

"Do it or you're dead."

The white nightshirt found its way through the iron bars. Just as Cody pulled it out a burst of machine-gun fire came at him from somewhere near the kitchen area. He felt a jolt of something red-hot hit him in the side and he fell to the ground.

Without aiming, he pulled the trigger on the laser gun and destroyed the kitchen.

He forced himself to a sitting position and crawled under a nearby truck. The compound was in chaos. The soldiers who were still alive were running everywhere, trying to escape the intermittent explosions. Jake had set at least one plastic explosive under every building in the camp except for the prisoners' barracks.

Cody wondered about the prisoners. He hoped Toni had seen the first explosion and flown in to rescue them.

Before he blacked out Cody had one last thought. It was, oddly enough, about Rachel. It would have been nice to see her again. She was a good friend.

CHAPTER 17

The flies buzzed around his wounds and refused to give him any peace. Cody finally opened his eyes and discovered that it was midmorning. From his hiding place under the burned-out truck he could see that there wasn't much left of the camp.

All the vehicles had been destroyed and any soldiers who had lived through the attack had fled on foot.

Cody was amazed that he was still alive. Now that it was daylight he could see where he'd been hit. A large chunk of flesh had been torn out of his side. Fortunately the wound had crusted over with blood during the night.

It hurt to move but he knew he had no choice. Once the CCR received news of the raid it would send troops out in force.

A water faucet was sticking out of the ground near the end of the truck. Cody crawled to it and turned the valve, letting the cold water wash over his face. Then he drank his fill.

Painfully he inched to his feet, slung his gun on his good side and started walking through the smoke and debris.

Charred bodies littered the ground around him. Most of the buildings were flattened and the guard towers no longer existed. Nothing but pieces was left of the building where he used to attend indoctrination classes.

He walked to the children's barracks and threw open the door. It was empty except for the cots. He slit one of the mattresses and ripped off its thin cotton covering to use as bandages and protection from the sun.

Outside he looked around for something he could carry that would hold water. But there was nothing.

The last time he had left the prison camp he'd gone out a narrow tunnel in the dead of night and escaped through the torturous desert. This time he would leave in broad daylight through what was left of the front gate and take the road. The CCR wouldn't be looking for one person and if he heard a patrol he could always get off the road and hide.

His steps were labored and he knew he wasn't making very good time. About a mile from camp he was wishing he'd looked harder for something to hold water.

It dawned on him that he hadn't gone back to check on Sidoron. He chuckled and the effort made him cough. "I sure wouldn't want to be in the colonel's place when half the Republic army shows up and finds him locked in that cage without his clothes."

A slight breeze blew and there were a few clouds overhead. Cody was grateful. He sat down on the side of the road to rest and noticed that his wound had broken open and was bleeding.

He sighed. "I don't even know where I'm going. Jake and the others are probably safe at the rebel base by now. The camp by the sand dunes has most likely been disassembled now that the brass has their shipment of trilithium.

"Maybe I'll go east. That's it. I've never seen that part of the country." He lay down on his side in the dirt. I'll get started as soon as I rest awhile—did I say that out loud or did I think it? It doesn't matter. Nothing matters. . . .

CHAPTER 18

"I've had this dream before." Cody moaned.

This was just like the time with Rachel, when he'd been shot in the shoulder and dreamed that Toni had found him in her chopper.

But this time it seemed so real. He could hear other people talking too and he even thought he heard a familiar bark.

"Wait a minute. Mike wasn't in my dream." His eyes fluttered open and he saw Jake Christmas leaning over him. Cody's eyes closed again. "You're not supposed to be here," he muttered, and then he dozed off to the whirring of chopper blades.

The next time he opened his eyes he felt something cold and wet on his forehead. He reached up to touch it. It was a towel.

Cody frowned. "I must be hallucinating again." He looked to the side and discovered he was in some sort of hospital ward. There were rows of white beds beside him; some of them held patients.

It didn't make sense. If the CCR had found him, they would probably have shot him on the spot. This had to be an American hospital.

He tried to sit up. A roaring, searing pain shot through his side, seemed to take his whole body.

"Hey, cut that out, soldier. How are you going to get well if you tear out all your stitches?"

"Toni?"

"Who else?" The smiling brunette sat gently on the edge of his bed. "We were about to give up on you. The doctor said you'd lost too much blood and he didn't expect you to live."

"But *I* told him you were too ornery to let a little thing like a bullet get you down." Jake stood over Cody, grinning.

"So it's true. My dream about the chopper really happened."

Toni smiled. "You didn't think we would leave you out there, did you?"

"Major McLaughlin and some other fliers met us right on schedule that night at the prison camp. But by the time we figured out you weren't with the prisoners it was too late. We had to get them to safety."

"So they made it out all right?"

"Every last one of them," Jake said proudly. "The doctors here at the base are helping them to get back to normal physically and then they'll be taken to the mountains, where they can begin to live their lives again."

"How's Trisha?"

"She's going to be fine. She has a couple of cracked ribs but the swelling has gone down." Jake moved to the door. "In fact, she's been waiting to see you, along with several other concerned members of G Company."

Cody pulled the towel off and raised his head to watch Jake open the door. Nick, Trisha, Matt, Slick, Davey, Patch and the Smiths trooped in. A furry blur raced past them and eagerly put his paws up on the bed.

"Hello, Mike." Cody reached out to stroke his head.

"I've been taking good care of him, Cody." Davey exclaimed.

"I know you have. Thanks."

Trisha moved to the end of the bed. "I don't know how to say this, Cody . . . but if you hadn't come when you did . . . well . . ."

Cody felt uncomfortable. "It wasn't just me. Jake and the others had a big part in it."

"That's right," Nick chimed in. "Don't go giving him all the credit or he'll get a big head. Here." He laid some wilted yellow flowers on Cody's chest. "We brought you these. Course, they looked better a few days ago."

"Here, here. What's all this racket about?" A large nurse marched in, clapping her hands.

"The doctor has *not* okayed any visitors for this young man. Everybody has to leave immediately."

"Atten-tion!"

Jake and Toni both jumped to their feet and executed rigid salutes.

"Colonel Wyman would like to have a word with Mr. Pierce." An aide cleared the aisle so that the intimidating commanding officer could get through.

Matt grabbed Patch and Davey and pulled them out of the way.

The tall silver-haired man walked up to the side of Cody's bed, took his hat off and shoved it under his arm. "I heard you were awake, so I came right over. I don't believe in beating around the bush, son, so I'll get right to it. The last time you and I talked I treated you poorly. I assumed that because of your age you couldn't be of any assistance to the United States Army. I was wrong. Dead wrong.

"Reports have reached me that you have participated in an unprecedented number of victorious raids against the enemy. And that you have on numerous occasions risked your life in the service of your country."

He turned to the aide and took a small blue cloth-covered box from his hands. "I hope you will not be offended that this medal isn't a new one. Until we have regained our country I'm afraid it will have to do." The colonel reached down and pinned the shiny silver emblem on the front of Cody's hospital gown, then stepped back.

"Ladies and gentlemen, will you join me in saluting the recipient of our nation's medal of heroism and bravery?"

Everyone in the room, including the patients who were able, proudly raised their hands to their foreheads. Then the colonel led them in a round of applause.

"Speech," Slick yelled. "Speech."

Cody touched the medal reverently. "I . . . don't know what to say. . . ."

"I hope you'll say yes, son. Your country needs you. When you're feeling better, I have a special assignment for you under the joint command of Majors McLaughlin and Christmas."

Cody glanced around the room at the sea of smiling friendly faces. Suddenly the thought of Rachel popped into his head again. He nodded slowly. "Until we win. Then I've got some other business that needs doing. . . ."

About the Author

GARY PAULSEN is the distinguished author of many critically acclaimed books for young people, including three Newbery Honor books: *The Winter Room*, *Hatchet* and *Dogsong*. His novel *The Haymeadow* received the Western Writers of America Golden Spur Award. Among his newest Delacorte Press books are *Alida's Song* (a companion to *The Cookcamp*), *Brian's Return* and *Brian's Winter* (companions to *Hatchet*), *Soldier's Heart*, *The Transall Saga*, *My Life in Dog Years*, *Sarny: A Life Remembered* (a companion to *Nightjohn*), *The Schernoff Discoveries*, *Father Water, Mother Woods: Essays on Fishing and Hunting in the North Woods* and five books about Francis Tucket's adventures in the Old West. Gary Paulsen has also published fiction and nonfiction for adults, as well as picture books created with his wife, the painter Ruth Wright Paulsen. The Paulsens live in New Mexico and on the Pacific Ocean.